FOR YOU

And now abide faith, hope and love, these three, but the greatest of these is love. Cor 13:13

PROPOSALTUDE

PROPOSALTUDE

Prologue

"You are stupid! Where did you get your medical credentials from?" yelled an angry, drug-addicted musician.

"I will be out of here within twenty-four hours…you better bring me my stuff, or I will call security on you!" The musician hollered.

"I don't care who you call, you have been signed into my care, and it's your choice. If you want to die, get up and walk out of here!" The resident doctor stated quietly as she glared at her favorite pop icon.

"Am I supposed to be impressed because of who you are? You are in this program because you are an addict…you almost died from an overdose. Unbelievable, I want to help you get better, but if you continue with your nasty attitude, no one will care if you fail. There will be no more Keith Michaels! What do you want me to put on your death certificate?" Dr. Childs stated coldly.

Dr. Destiny Childs shook her head at Michaels. Keith Michaels glared at her. He was a mega star. When he barked commands, people catered to his every whim. No one had ever been so blunt. He looked away from her in an angry stare. Dr. Childs watched Keith Michaels' body language. Dr. Childs returned his stare with an icy, agitated look.

Dr. Destiny Childs continued to look at him and stated, "The choice is yours. You choose!"

Destiny slammed the door of the detox room and breathed a sigh of relief. Movie stars, musicians, and politicians all acted the same when they were in a detoxification program. Designer, cocaine, marijuana or prescription drugs all had the same reaction to the addict. The addiction overpowers the addict and consumes the addict's normal life. The addict is immune to the feelings of others and turns into a selfish, needy infant that harms themselves and alienates family and friends. It was amazing how money could buy anybody or anything, she pledged to herself that money would not tempt her. She took a Hippocratic Oath, and her patients came first, even if they were spoiled, wealthy rock stars.

"Hey, Destiny, how was Mister Goody Two Shoes? Did he threaten to have you killed, too?" asked Dr. Charles, her colleague at the France Recovery Detoxification Center.

"No, he threatened to call security on me." Destiny smiled as she charted her notes and gave the nurse her orders for Keith Michaels.

"I'm disappointed. Of all the people to come through our doors, I would have never imagined Keith Michaels. I looked up to him," Dr. Charles remarked with disappointment in his voice.

"We all have demons to purge. Before this fellowship, I used to think of famous people as Greek gods. I've learned they are plagued with deep, underlying issues, and the drugs dull the pain. The difference between us, and famous people is we live in the real world, and their world is fantasy. They live behind the facade of glitz and glamour. Have a good night, Peter. See you in the morning." Destiny smiled as she walked to the staff locker room and changed her clothes.

She stepped on the scale and frowned. A whopping 177 lbs., this job of curing other people of their demons was affecting her weight and stressing her out. Destiny was determined to fight the weight battle and get her life back on track. The world saw Destiny's body as the epitome of the black woman's shape. She had no stomach or back fat, nice, toned derriere that most women would pay for. Destiny saw a fat chick with no hope of being in a loving relationship.

Dr. Jefferson walked into the room, he watched Dr. Childs as she stared at her silhouette in the mirror. She was a beautiful milk chocolate specimen of a woman. He was amazed at her beauty and poise. She had charisma that made people love her instantly. She was an excellent doctor, and Dr. Destiny Childs had a good heart. Her charisma was infectious. He wondered why Destiny was still single.

"Oh...you startled me...I 'm sorry if I was in your way," she stammered as she quickly moved away from the full -length mirror.

"No problem, I was just admiring your ...uh...your strength, I mean," Dr. Jefferson added sheepishly. He could not believe how easily it had come out of his mouth.

Destiny smiled. "What do you mean?" she asked as she grabbed her keys and stared into his gray eyes.

"Well, do you have time after work? We can go for a coffee," Dr. Jefferson flirted. He felt bold and hoped she would bite. He normally was not attracted to milk chocolate African American women, but Richard Jefferson desired and needed to be in Destiny's presence.

"Wow! Dr. Jefferson, are you sure??! I mean...you know that I am...African American. The most hated specimen in society," she stammered. Destiny smiled as her heart skipped a beat. She was surprised. Destiny was attracted to Richard, but she dismissed his offer as being cordial. Destiny crinkled her forehead.

"If I did not have to pick up my child, I would take you up on your offer, because this is an historic event. I promise I will not tell. It will be our little secret," Dr. Childs stated playfully as she walked away.

He was shocked. He was more impressed than ever. She had a child, and she managed to make it through medical school!

Destiny picked up her son, and they went home. Her son was five years old, and she was a single mother. Not by choice, but she figured she had made the wrong choices in men. Never again will she make that mistake. She checked her messages; nothing new. She sighed and fell asleep in front of the television.

"Dr. Childs, I am so glad you are here, our spoiled megastar is howling for you. What is it about you? Everyone misses you when you are not here," her best friend of fifteen years stated.

"The same thing they say about you Shannon, when you are not here," Destiny retorted as she looked over the megastar's file.

"How much Demerol did Dr. Orleans write for him?" asked Dr. Childs.

"He stated that nothing was wrong with what you had prescribed, but the star said he was in pain. He had a severe fracture, and he has a high threshold for pain medication," Shannon reiterated as she relayed the message.

Destiny smiled as she went into the room with the superstar.

"Where have you been!!? I thought you were supposed to be my doctor?" he stated as he slurred.

"Remember, you kicked me out. Now why are you yelling for me? I am not going to increase your dosage; actually, I think it would be better if we put you on a regiment of no medications at all," Destiny stated as she examined him.

"So, what is your real name?" she paused as she looked at his pupils. "Who has been giving you pills?" She looked disgusted. She checked the chart and noticed the same visitor in the nurse's notes daily. "You still look high; I think I am going to stop your family visits for a while. Do you understand what I am saying?" Destiny asked.

Mr. Keith Michaels had fallen asleep, and Destiny stared at his emaciated body. This was his last chance; if this drug intervention did not work, he would be dead. There was a knock at the door.

"Hi," Dr. Jefferson stated shyly. "Making sure you were okay in here. Earlier, Keith Michaels was hitting people and crying for you. What did you do?" asked an astonished Dr. Jefferson.

"Maybe if we put him on a protein diet and slowly eliminate his addiction, get him to exercise, he might just make it," Destiny suggested, ignoring his comment.

"Okay Doctor, let's try it. I will sign off on it. You put in your resignation, why? I thought you liked it here?" Dr. Jefferson inquired.

"I do, but I am ready to go back to the United States," she stated as she eyed the chiseled, bronze skin of Dr. Jefferson. He was about six feet two, and fit well into his Armani slacks and black buttoned Marc Jacobs Polo shirt. She saw his pectoral muscles protrude through his thin tee shirt. Destiny sighed and smiled half-heartedly. He would never look at her that way. He probably was married to a beautiful French model.

Dr. Jefferson looked at Destiny. He wondered what she was thinking.

Dr. Jefferson began apologetically, "Look, I know I can be very mean, and if you are leaving on my account, I'm sorry. I, uh, do not have the best bedside manner. I mean, I can be an ass." Dr. Jefferson wanted to take her in his arms and kiss her passionately.

Destiny sighed dreamingly as she thought about his ass. He looked toned, and the thought of grabbing him into her was pure ecstasy.

"No, Dr. Jefferson, it is not you. I have to stop running away from my past," Destiny stated as she brushed past Dr. Jefferson and continued her rounds. As she walked down the hall, she felt his piercing stare. Destiny felt she did not have a chance with him; he was sexy and wealthy.

"Hi, Dr. Childs. Why were you flirting with Dr. Jefferson?" asked an inquisitive old lady.

Dr. Childs smiled. "Was I really, he just asked me why I was leaving." Nancy looked at Destiny in disbelief.

"In all my years, when a man asks why are you leaving and apologizes for being mean, that man is interested in you!" The head nurse practically yelled at the top of her lungs.

Destiny looked at Nancy. She was a beautiful, tall brunette, probably in her sixties, but she looked like she was forty. She was the best head nurse Destiny had ever seen. Not only did Nurse Nancy bark orders, she was highly skilled in all procedures and quicker than any other nurse on her feet.

"Yeah, right! Men are not interested in me. All they want to do is have sex with me and keep me in their Rolodex for later. He probably sees me as his latest conquest," Destiny stated as she thought about Tony back in the states. Maybe this time they could make it work. Destiny was ready to settle down.

"I'm no fool, anybody can see the electricity you two put off when you are in the room together. Destiny...stop running from your destiny. I've known Richard for a long time; he's a good man... he really likes you. Can you promise me one thing? When he approaches you, you will be open and receive it," Nancy stated lovingly. Nancy had come to love Destiny in the two years she had worked at the facility. She was an excellent doctor and did not depend on her looks to get her through her studies.

"Okay, Nurse Nancy. I will do just that...but I'm sure he will not even ask," Destiny stated just as Dr. Richard Jefferson walked up to the lunch bench.

"Do you usually eat lunch here?" Dr. Jefferson asked.

Destiny looked up into his gray eyes. She smiled as she tried to gain her composure. Nurse Nancy winked at her as she left the couple in their discourse.

"Only when I have stalkers," she stated playfully.

Richard frowned. "Ooh, is it that obvious?" Richard laughed. Destiny was impressed with his laugh. His whole face lit up, and the muscles in his abdomen relaxed to reveal a toned, fit six-pack. Destiny was sure he was in his late thirties. Damn, thought Destiny, this man is the perfect male Adonis! The sun beamed down on his sandy brown hair. Destiny had to look away before he recognized her labored breathing. She closed her eyes and imagined him and her in the bedroom. She believed it would be deliciously exquisite. Destiny bit her bottom lip as she erased the wicked thought from her mind. A strong baritone voice whispered in her ear.

"You shouldn't bite your lip like that." Destiny opened her eyes to see Richard kneeling in front of her and gazing deep into her eyes. As their eyes met, two lonely people connected. It was a moment in time as both individuals studied one another. He grabbed her hand tightly. Destiny felt euphoric as she dreamed that this fine specimen of a man was hers. Destiny begun to feel lightheaded and blurted out, "Why, want to taste my lips?" She encouraged Dr. Jefferson with her eyes.

He did not answer as he pulled Destiny closer to him. He began to caress her arms. He kissed her hand and rubbed her check. He slowly tilted her chin, parted her lips, and his tongue hungrily met hers. As they kissed, the loneliness melted away in Destiny. She pulled him closer to her, trying to taste the very essence of his soul. It had been a long time since she felt a man's touch; it felt good. As they continued to kiss, she could smell the scent of DKNY Red on him. He gripped the sides of her waist passionately and held her tightly.

The more Destiny pulled him into her, the deeper his kisses got. He was sure the staff had become an audience.

He wanted to make her feel good; he did not want her to leave. Her kisses were electrifying. Neither one of them wanted to part from each other. As the kiss finally came to an end, they could not look at each other. Slowly, as they finally parted, he held her in his arms. Destiny reluctantly released herself from his grasp.

Richard looked down and away. "I'm sorry, I should not have lost control liked that. Please forgive me," he said as he stood and walked away.

Destiny whispered under her breath, "Please don't go." Destiny stared at the grass as the staff resumed their activities.

"Are you seeing Dr. Jefferson?" her best friend said, running behind her.

"No, I honestly do not know how that transpired," Destiny whispered in disbelief. She had just locked lips with Dr. Jefferson. "All of a sudden, I was in his big, strong arms. I am so embarrassed. You think he is going to fire me?" Destiny asked, concerned. Although she was becoming an expert in her field, she still needed the money and experience to take care of her son Alex.

"Probably, but from that kiss, he wants something more. That kiss was incredible. I've never seen Mr. Playboy do that before," Shannon stated playfully. Destiny looked worried.

"Really, Shannon...it felt so good, and right. As if a man could really love me? His lips were so soft, inviting. He smelled so good. I never thought I... uh...needed a man's touch like that. He gave me chills," Destiny breathlessly said. Destiny slowly stood up and went inside the clinic.

Destiny kept to herself, finished her rounds, and was on her way out when Shannon cornered her.

"So how long have you and Jeff been an item?" Shannon inquired.

"We are not!" Destiny exclaimed.

"Then what are you? because that kiss on the lawn proved otherwise," Shannon angrily said.

Shannon was mad that her friend had chosen to keep this relationship from her. They shared everything.

"I am hurt, Destiny…you could have told me. I would have not said a word," Shannon continued to talk.

"Shannon, shut up…I am not with Jefferson...today, I don't know what happened out there! All I know is that it felt good and I would not mind being with him. You don't believe me? We already had this discussion. But Tony called, he wants to try again, and I think I owe it to my son to be with his dad," Destiny said as she grabbed her keys.

"No, you don't. You need a man who is going to take care of you, love you the right way. Not someone who is between wives and only wants to have sex with you. There is a statement, if you continue to do something the same way, you keep getting the same results. Leave Tony alone, revoke your resignation, and see where this thing with Dr. Jefferson leads," Shannon urged.

Destiny smiled. "I think we were both fatigued. That is why we kissed. Trust me; I'm sure he did not mean it." Destiny picked up her son, Alex, and went home. At dinner, Alex rambled on about the great day he had. Destiny looked interested as he talked, but she kept thinking about the kiss she shared with Richard.

She drifted off to sleep and dreamed of Richard. He begun by telling her he wanted to love her passionately. He embraced her and whispered in her ear.

"I always thought you were beautiful," he whispered as he gently bit her earlobe. Next, he travelled to meet her lips. He gently guided her bottom lip into his mouth. He sucked on it.

"You taste sweet and good," he said as he continued exploring Destiny's body with his tongue and lips.

"I want your mind," he slurred as he kissed the imaginary line between her voluptuous breasts. Richard was in heaven as he continued on his journey.

"I want you to love me with your heart," he said softly as he kissed her stomach and stopped at the entrance to her womanhood.

"Destiny, I want you to love me with your heart, mind, and body." He looked up. He searched her face for any objections. Destiny stood looking down at his face. She wanted this man to take her right now. She pushed his face into her womanhood, hoping he would oblige.

Richard stood up. "Wait a minute, I have a gift for you," he said as he scooped her up in his arms and took her to his bedroom. He laid her on the bed and retrieved the bright red oblong box from the cherry wood dresser.

Destiny squealed with excitement as she opened the box. Inside the box was a pair of purple panties.

"Richard, they are beautiful!!!! How did you know they are my favorite color?" Destiny squealed excitedly.

"Put them on," Richard urged. "And undress in front of me," he demanded.

Destiny seductively rose from the bed. She let her pants fall effortlessly down until they hit the floor. She took off her shirt. She put the purple panties on and noticed a weird sensation. Richard pulled Destiny to him.

"Tonight, I am going to make passionate love to you," he said as the panties started to vibrate. He laid Destiny on the bed and caressed her body with his tongue. The vibrating panties had three speeds. While Richard was kissing her innermost parts, the panties went slow…then they would speed up, and then slow again. Destiny began to breathe faster and keep rhythm with the panties, until finally she felt Richard enter her.

"Ooh!" Destiny yelled as she could not contain herself. Richard expertly slid in and out while the crotch less vibrating panties continued pulsating. Destiny grabbed Richard's ass, gripped him firmly as she gyrated her hips under him.

"Oh, Richard, I needed this!" Destiny yelled.

Destiny jumped up. She looked at the time. It was two o'clock in the morning. She felt wet between her legs.

What an amazing dream! She stood up and went to the bathroom. She was so embarrassed to have a dream like that; she could not look herself in the mirror. She had to find out about these vibrating panties. It had been so long since she was intimate, she was unaware of all the sex toys on the market. Destiny was not sure if vibrating panties existed, and what were they supposed to do. If they were anything like the dream, she had to get some. If Destiny was bold enough, she would have to take Dr. Jefferson up on his offer of coffee. Her dream felt so amazing. If only Tony would treat her like that. Oh well, Destiny thought as she checked on her son and went back to sleep. Destiny awoke to a loud thump at the door.

"Good morning, I have a delivery for Dr. Childs," stated the deliveryman.

"Oh, thank you," she replied as she tipped him.

Destiny looked at the envelope. Maybe it was from Tony. Maybe this time he was apologizing and they would get back together. She quickly opened the envelope.

I'm not sorry about the kiss.

You've been on my mind,

Let me prepare dinner for you

I'm curious, want to know

What would have happened, had the location been right?

I'm attracted to you!

Richard

Destiny smiled as she read the note over again. Maybe she should try and get to know Dr. Jefferson better. She had never dated an older man before. She was touched that Richard Jefferson was interested in her. Should she say yes? Destiny wondered what the ramifications would be if she accepted. Destiny imagined wild, erotic thoughts of Richard. The phone rang as she finished her daydream.

"Hello," the voice stated on the other end of the phone.

"Hi," Destiny responded.

"Did you get my flowers?" he asked.

"Yes...thank you," she stated as her heart begun to beat faster.

"So, can I prepare dinner for you?" asked the persistent male.

"Okay, when?" Destiny stated, feeling brave.

"What about tomorrow night? Give you time to find a babysitter," Richard stated.

"You are so considerate. Ok, it is a date. Where do I meet you?" asked Destiny.

"I will pick you up at 8 p.m.," he said and hung up.

"Mommy, look, Daddy sent you and me a letter," Alex said as he came in from the mailbox.

He gave both letters to his mom and sat down as she read his letter. At least Tony was a better father than a boyfriend or husband. After she gave Alex his note and the picture his father drew, she read the one he wrote to her. Destiny was so touched by his words. She picked up the phone and called him in New York City.

"Hello," answered a soft, whispery voice. Destiny's heart fell. She cleared her throat to speak. No words would come out of her mouth.

"Hello," the voice stated again impatiently.

"Uh, hi, may I speak with Tony?" Destiny stated as she fought back the tears that were burning in her watery eyes.

"Hi, Destiny..." Tony answered breathlessly.

"I received your letter today...I guess you did not mean it? Still playing your old tricks...I'm stupid for believing that you could ever change," Destiny stated, trying to remain calm. She knew Tony hated when Destiny was cool as a cucumber. He never knew what to expect.

"Des, look, baby, I love you more than life itself. Just that right now my life is complicated. I did mean everything I wrote, and one day it will be you and me. I promise!!!" Tony whispered.

"Why are you whispering? So, your latest conquest won't hear you are no good?! Why are you begging? Trying to save me when things don't work out?" She paused as she tried to fight the burning sensation in her heart.

"Don't bother, Tony...I am done." She hung the phone up in his face.

She went to the bathroom to cry. Where was that strong and intelligent lady now? She wished she had a solid relationship with her mother. She could cry on her shoulders. Her mother was not a loving person. She just had to bear it. She could call Shannon. This was Shannon's day off. She usually spent it with her husband and children. Destiny did not want to bother her with her troubles. Shannon could not stand Tony. She said he was no good. Destiny washed her face and decided she was going to spend a family day with Alex. She had to stop thinking about Tony.

Destiny and Alex retrieved their bikes and rode to the park.

"Mommy, look, no hands!" Alex smiled as he glided through the park as fast as he could. Destiny raced past him as they continued their ride.

"Mommy wins, by a bike slide." She laughed as they parked the bikes by the duck pond.

"Dr. Childs..." said a surprised Dr. Jefferson. He knew her physique anywhere.

Destiny looked up, surprised to see her dream lover standing in front of her. Destiny blushed as she could see the imprint of his muscles and other items through his biking attire. She tried to ignore his bulging manhood. He caught her gaze and smiled, as if to say come and get me.

"Dr. Jefferson...you ride your bike here often?" she said, regaining her composure.

"Actually, I do. I have to keep in shape...if I want to be with you, you know my age and all," he stated coyly.

"Really?! Dr. Jefferson, you can get anyone you choose...don't you have a harem?" Destiny decided to flirt and play along. Being in Dr. Jefferson's presence gave her an energy surge. She perused the pond to keep an eye on Alex; he was busy making friends with a little boy about his age.

"I don't think so, cause if that is the case...why are you not my wife?" he said firmly, looking into her eyes.

Dr. Jefferson's statement caught her off guard. Destiny stared back. She was searching his eyes, looking for answers. His beautiful gray eyes stared back.

As Destiny was about to answer, Richard pulled her to him, and he passionately kissed her.

"Destiny, I thought love at first sight was purely scientific. But since I have been in your presence, you have made a believer out of me." He paused to see if Destiny was still with him.

"I know you feel the same way. I can't promise you it will be easy, but I can make you and Alex happy. Marry me," Richard Jefferson stated huskily.

He knew what he just did was unorthodox and tacky, but he wanted Destiny to know how he felt about her. It was painful to see this woman leave without her knowing his true feelings. Destiny stared at him in disbelief.

"You want to m-m-marry me-e?" she stuttered like a little girl. Her heart began racing. She blinked her eyes rapidly. The sky started spinning around her. Her body swayed as Richard's strong body caught her. The scent of

Richard felt soothing and calming. He held her in his arms until she came through.

"For a minute, I was going to give you mouth-to-mouth resuscitation," he said, concerned, as he checked to see if Destiny was lucid.

"Do you really want to marry me?" Destiny pinched herself to make sure she was not dreaming.

"Yes. I know the proposal sounds ludicrous, but I love you. And I am not as old as you think. I'm only 40." He winked. She smiled and buried her head in his neck. Destiny was shocked at the safety and security of his touch.

She looked at Richard for the first time. He was gentle and kind. His heart was pure.

"I guess I better put you down; little man is looking at me, wondering why I am holding his mom." He smiled as he gently let her go.

"Let me take care of you," he pleaded.

"Are you sure?" Destiny asked.

She motioned to Alex to let him know she was okay.

"Dr. Jefferson, I'm damaged... I'm still in love with my ex," Destiny blurted out.

Richard looked at her, incredulous. He shook his head.

"Is he still in love with you?" He paused. "Because you have been here two years, I've never seen him here. If you were the mother of my child, I would have never let you go," he stated dryly.

Destiny felt stupid after she revealed her feelings. Why did she always have to mess things up? She folded her arms as Richard's gaze burnt through her very soul. She nervously looked around.

"That is the problem with men, they play the role that they are a player, but when they find the real thing, they damage it and think that they can always come back," he remarked.

Richard stared at Destiny, waiting for an explanation. She shifted her feet from left to right; any other man would have left or cursed her out. She could not understand why this man was still watching and studying her.

"I have to go," Destiny stated as she fought back the

tears. She did not know how to change the subject or mask her true feelings. She went to her son, and they rode away. As she pedaled faster, she still could feel his gray eyes piercing her in her back.

Richard watched as she pedaled furiously away. He replayed the scene in his mind. He thought maybe he should have made small talk instead of blurting out his feelings. A weird idea crossed his mind. He would buy her a naughty girl gift.

At the apartment, Destiny went to the bathroom and cried her eyes out. If she never married, at least she had a taste of pure love. If her feelings for Richard were infatuation, she would forever embrace her fantasy. It was probably just two lonely people looking for love in the wrong place.

Destiny put Alex to bed and turned on the television. She heard a light tap on the door. She peeked through the peephole. Oh my gosh, it's Richard Jefferson. She wondered what did he want at this hour.

"Destiny, open up...I promise I'm not a stalker. I want to apologize," he kindly stated.

Destiny opened the door and invited him in.

"Look, maybe I was too forward earlier...maybe I scared you? I do want to marry you...if you want, I will wait...but if you are getting back with your ex, I wish you good luck." He reached inside his coat pocket.

"Let me help you decide," Richard stated as he pulled out a red little wrapped box. Destiny unwrapped the present to reveal a purple pair of vibrating panties. She smiled, kissed, and embraced Richard.

Destiny was not sure where a life with Richard would lead, but she was willing to take the risk. Destiny smiled as she led Richard to her bedroom.

LOVETUDE

LOVETUDE

.

The assistant placed the Cosmo cream from DrugCo on the vanity table for the television evangelist. The television evangelist was very vain. People always remarked how beautiful her skin was. She had been using Cosmo cream for twenty years. She smiled as she applied the cream and was escorted to the stage by Candace Wellingcamp.

"Hello, New York Ladies of Christ!" the televangelist yelled as she felt a sharp, stabbing pressure against her left cheek. The television evangelist fell to the ground yelling, "Oh GOD!!! OH GOD!!! Help me!"

The audience in Madison Square Garden stared in disbelief. Most people thought it was part of the presentation. The television evangelist always used theatrics to compel people to come to Christ. The crowd in the arena went silent. The television evangelist's face oozed with deep purple blisters; that had white puss and blood squirting out from her face. The blood shot out like a super soaker water gun into the crowd. The television station cut to a commercial, and the medics rushed to assist the television evangelist.

Pastor Candace Wellingcamp stared in amazement. Candace looked around; she did not hear a gunshot. Candace continued to scan the room when blood landed on her cream-colored business suit and something hit her in the back of her head. Pandemonium broke out as people began to run for the exits and other women in the crowd begin to mimic the same symptoms as the television evangelist. Candace rubbed the back of her head and reached for her phone in her pocket. She immediately dialed 911. Candace winced as she heard the voice of the Lord tell her go to the stage and reassure the crowd so the authorities could help the people in agony.

Even though Candace was a pastor, she had a hard time speaking in front of crowds. She wished she was a gifted orator like her best friend Kareer. She breathed deeply and began her plea.

"Children of God, now is the time to extend our love by being calm, and help our brothers and sisters that are in pain or scared. Has anyone read Lovetude? At this moment, we must have an attitude of love; willing to help our Christian family. Please return to your seats. Remember, God has not given us the spirit of fear, but a sound mind, and a heart to display love." At the sound of Pastor Wellingcamp's voice, the chaos stopped; the police, paramedics, and convention staff took care of the injured.

Kareer listened to the radio as she drove through the Denver, Colorado, traffic to pick up her children from school. Kareer slammed on the brakes of her Ford Explorer as the sport utility vehicle came to a screeching stop. She beat the steering wheel with her hands as the radio announced that the State of New York had filed criminal charges against DrugCo for the mayhem that had taken place at Madison Square Garden, and the facial disfigurement of people all over the world. Kareer's hand began to shake as she dialed the New York office of DrugCo. Why hadn't her boss called her? Kareer shook her head as his phone went straight to voicemail. Kareer arrived at her children's school and turned up the radio to hear the reports about DrugCo. People had been disfigured by Cosmo, an anti-aging face cream manufactured by DrugCo, the company she worked for. Oh no, thought Kareer, why hadn't her office called?

A statement had to be made to reassure the public. Kareer anxiously waited for the phone call from DrugCo. She immediately checked her phone for any emergency emails. Kareer tried to call the main office in New York, but all circuits were busy. As the twins put their stuff in the trunk of her Ford Explorer, her phone rang.

"Kareer, this is Buchanan. We need you on the next flight to New York," her boss barked into the phone. Kareer Matthews was the chief public relations officer of DrugCo. She was perturbed; she should have been notified as soon as DrugCo was named liable.

"How long have you known about the situation?" Kareer asked as she put the phone on speaker and told the twins to stop fighting.

There was a long silence on the other end. Buchannan did not know how to tell his publicist they had known for months and were being blackmailed. Instead, he told her he had emailed the investigation report. Kareer sighed in disbelief. She knew Buchannan was lying. Her mind started working fast as she began to pen the public relations speech in her mind.

She swooped into her two- story home's driveway and went upstairs to her office to work on a statement to the press. She noticed the Caller id read Pastor Candace Wellingcamp. Most people would not understand their connection. Hell, sometimes Kareer and Candace did not either. They had accepted their differences and become best friends. Love and forgiveness was the true theme of Candace and Kareer's lovetude.

Past

Kareer reminisced on how she met Candace. Kareer's oldest set of twins had just turned twelve, and Melissa came into the kitchen and watched her mom put up the dishes in the cabinet.

"Mom, I thought you said Daddy had a business trip and he couldn't celebrate with us, on our birthday?" Melissa asked curiously.

"He did," Kareer stated, not paying attention to her little girl.

"Mom, are we getting a divorce? Because I saw Daddy with a blonde hair lady and they were kissing on the lips." Melissa stated indignantly. Kareer dropped the glass out of her hand, and it hit the floor. Scott her husband, came into the kitchen to see what had happened. Kareer knew he had been philandering, but never so close to home. She quickly tried to think up an excuse.

"Are you sure? Maybe it was Mr. Piedmont; you know they always mistake your daddy for him. Besides,

Daddy only has eyes for me," Kareer stated as she went and kissed Scott on the lips. Scott played along, not exactly sure what had happened. Melissa made a snickering sound and ran out of the kitchen yelling,

"Yuck!!! Mom and Dad, you guys are gross." Kareer motioned Scott to follow her into the office and closed the door behind him. Scott followed, wondering what he had done this time. Kareer glared at him.

"I know about the affairs, the women. All I asked you to do is not bring them in my house or be seen in Denver by your peers or children!" she yelled at the top of her lungs. She did not care if the whole suburb of Northern Denver heard her.

"Your daughter saw you with her," Kareer stated between sobs. Dammit, she thought as she bit her lip. She hated when she cried. People mistook her crying for weakness when she was angry. She would have thrown the phone at Scott's face if it was not attached to the wall.

"You go in there and fix it with your daughter," Kareer demanded.

Scott did not understand why Kareer was so upset. She knew that their marriage was a farce. He married her because she was pregnant with his twins. When they first started dating, it was a sex thing. He did not want to abandon his children. Hell, he really did not like her. After all, she was an African American woman and he was a white man.

"You want the divorce now?" Scott asked, hoping she would say yes. He would never directly ask for one. He never knew his family; he was reared in a foster home.

"No, Scott. I just don't want our children seeing you with your women. I believe in marriage. I thought you did, too." She fought back the tears. "I guess I'm a fool, my lovetude does not exist. It's a figment of my imagination, because my dumb ass is in love with you." Kareer paused as she caught her breath. "You tell that bitch I won't divorce you! If I am miserable, all three of us will be miserable together!" Kareer yelled forcefully.

"Then you will be in a marriage by yourself. I will not stop seeing her, she is the love of my life. And if you had not gotten pregnant, it would have been me and her," Scott stated calmly as he looked straight in her eyes.

All of the strength she had mustered up to confront her husband evaporated. She felt defeated and heartbroken. She stared at him incredulously. She wanted to scratch his eyes out. Her husband of twelve years had told her he was in love with someone else. Her marriage was over. She turned and walked out of the office. She went up the stairs to the bedroom and cried herself to sleep.

A few hours later, Scott entered the bedroom and sat on the side of the bed by her feet. She pretended to be asleep. Scott rubbed her feet. He knew her weakness was her feet.

"Kareer, I know you are not sleep. I wanted to apologize to you. I never meant to hurt you. I love you as a friend…I'm angry with myself. I have Prostate cancer, and I only have six months to live. I wish I was a better husband. I wish I would have taken the Sunday sermons seriously, been a better father to our children." He paused as he watched the covers of the bed drape her body. Scott had to admit, Kareer was gorgeous, and all of his colleagues thought his wife was intelligent, smart and gorgeous. He thought maybe if he had tried to love her, then maybe things would have been different. Scott had a huge sexual appetite that Kareer could not fill.

"My colleagues do not understand how you are my wife. Your God must be punishing me for being so dishonorable to you." Scott continued babbling nervously. Scott watched as the cover stirred. Kareer's body shivered as Scott poured out his heart to her. Kareer fought the urge to turn and console her husband. Kareer desperately wanted to embrace her husband, tell him she loved him, and together they would fight his disease. The tears raced down her cheeks. She placed her hands over her mouth to stop the whimpering agony of pain emitting from her soul. Kareer decided to lie still. Scott had made a mockery of their marriage, he had been evil. He was going to have to deal with his issues alone.

"I'm sorry," he stated as he closed the door and went down the stairs.

Present

Kareer rubbed her eyes. She still had the same bedroom set. It was time to move on. Kareer had been living in a shell for so long, she was afraid to emerge. After this trip, she would do spring cleaning on the house and her life. Scott was gone, but the remnants of the marriage, hurt and deceit lingered in her abode. Kareer wondered where the time went. Had it been six years already? Kareer hoped she would be able to start living, and no longer existing.

"Mom, hurry up, you are going to be late for your flight'' exclaimed her eighteen-year-old son named Donovan. He had become a man as she watched him put her bags in the car. She was a little apprehensive about leaving her family as she went to work in New York. Kareer did not have a choice. It had been six years since her husband died from cancer. He left her with four children and a bankrupt business.

The entire family packed into the car and drove to Denver International Airport. She kissed her children goodbye and told them to be good. She went through the terminal and waited for the flight for New York City.

She hated flying, but her job provided the security and safety she needed after the death of her husband. She smiled when the flight attendant escorted her to first class. At least she would ride in comfort for the next six hours. She opened her computer and looked at the report and case filing. She had to convey to the public that DrugCo was not liable for the accusations. After all, DrugCo had been around for eighty years with no complaints.

"Good evening, Miss, what would you like to drink?" Kareer had not had a drink in years. She smiled demurely as she thought of a drink. She decided on a Long Island Iced Tea. Kareer chuckled, she ordered one of the strongest drinks on the menu. Kareer was not a drinker, all she'd ever done was sip. But this case was going to be difficult; she needed to adorn her punching gloves and suit up. Her career and life were on the line. Her best friend Candace had witnessed the Cosmo outbreak and was shaken up. When Kareer had heard about it, she had refused to believe that Cosmo was the culprit.

Kareer blinked twice as she continued reading the reports. It had to be a mistake. Kareer perused the briefs, her hands became sweaty and her heart raced. There was no way he could be employed by DrugCo. She noticed his name on the brief she was reading. Strange, she had not seen that name in twenty-three years. Amazing, her real love worked for the same company! She visualized how he would look now. He probably was married with a bunch of children, three ex-wives, a current live-in girlfriend, and a mistress. She smiled to herself as she downed the drink. The DrugCo situation was going to be a nightmare, but her heart was fluttering and dancing at the thought of seeing her love again. The drink had Kareer tipsy, and she fell into a fitful sleep.

Past

The ambulance rushed to the hospital. It had taken Kareer a long time, but she had finally convinced Scott to go to the hospital. She called the babysitter, Mrs. Moore, and followed Scott in her car. At the hospital, the physician on duty informed her it did not look good. She walked out of the room wondering who to call.

She fished in her purse for her phone. Instead of her phone, she picked up Scott's phone and dialed his mistress, Candace Blank.

"Scott, I told you, I can't do this anymore. It's not fair to me, her or you. Leave me alone, please. I am not strong enough to resist your charm," Candace stated as she secretly prayed, "Please Holy Spirit, break this urge, soul tie that has me in oppression to Scott."

"No Candace, it's Kareer, his wife. You need to come to the hospital. Scott is dying." Kareer hung up as she went back into the room with her husband.

"I'm sorry I couldn't love you like you needed to be loved. Promise me you will practice your lovetude and get your attitude of love back. There's a letter that came to the house five years ago. A Der…Gra it under..find it…." Scott was beginning to talk incoherently. He was slipping in and out of consciousness. He started saying more things, but she couldn't understand him. The machines began to scream, and instantly Kareer ran into the hallway and called for the nurse and doctor. Over the speaker she heard medical personnel call Code Blue, and doctors went running to stabilize him.

Candace was shaking as she got off the elevator. She had no idea why Scott's wife had called her. Candace hoped she was not about to be jumped by some big black gangsters. She had watched enough black movies to know that a black wife would never allow the mistress to see the lover at the hospital. Kareer eyed Candace as they met face to face for the first time. Candace nervously stared back at Kareer. She was beautiful, a chocolate milk complexion. Kareer's hair was pulled back in a ponytail to reveal a wrinkle-free face. Candace noticed Kareer was very curvy. She had the body of a video vixen. Candace cracked a semi-smile, Scott had exquisite taste, and Kareer was gorgeous. Kareer perused the face of Candace. She resembled Malibu Barbie. Kareer laughed; Scott was a connoisseur of all things elegant. Candace was the epitome of what every All-American male wanted. She was the All-American cheerleader dream date you would bring home to meet the family. At least Candace was not poor white trash. She looked like she had class. Kareer thought that had to be an oxymoron, because if she had class, she should have left her husband alone. Kareer breathed a sigh of melancholy as she broke the silence.

"He's in there," she said as she went to the waiting room.

Candace nodded as she walked into the hospital room. Candace stared at Scott's lifeless body. Candace made peace with Scott. It seemed like hours as she rationalized how to make peace with Kareer. Candace had to make peace with Kareer if God was to forgive her for her sin of fornication. Candace prayed and hoped that Scott had accepted Christ as his personal savior. Candace continued to pray that God would give her the strength to approach Kareer. Candace turned away from Scott's body and stared out the hospital room window. How did she get into this mess? Candace thought. Kareer should have been the secret mistress. After all, Candace was a prized possession. Every man wanted a piece of Candace. Besides, Candace thought the media and magazines always stated black women were ugly with their weaves, big asses, and dark, curly, nappy textured hair. Candace had a change of heart; she would not go talk to Kareer today.

He was already dead. There was nothing Candace could do. Kareer stared at the chair. She knew this day was coming. Kareer wished she had family to talk to, help her plan the funeral, or offer moral support. Scott had alienated her from her family years ago.

She sat in the chair, weak and defeated. Her husband of twelve years had checked out on her. The tears streamed down her face. Kareer put her hands in her lap and squeezed her eyes as tight as she could. She was unsure of what to do. Kareer missed Scott. She knew Scott was unfaithful to her, but he was her husband. As he neared the end of his life, she could have left him and biblically God would have forgiven her, but she had an agape and brotherly love for Scott.

Candace paused by the door of the waiting room. Candace watched as Kareer slumped into her seat. Candace felt her throat tighten. Candace had to admit, Kareer was a beautiful black woman. Scott had done well. She was a beautiful color of Nestle Quik chocolate milk mix.

Candace came out of the room and bolted for the elevator. Candace had been in love with Scott for so long, but the dead body on the gurney was not the man she had been in love with. The elevator opened, and Candace entered the small box. The door closed, and the elevator room went dark. The elevator room filled with white smoke, and a loud, deafening voice made her unable to move.

"GO BACK! YOU ARE THE ONLY FAMILY SHE HAS. YOU NEED HER, AND SHE NEEDS YOU!" the voice stated.

Candace laughed. "Yeah, right; remember, I am the mistress. I am the last person she would want to see,"

Candace replied. As Candace played with the buttons, she began to hear Pastor Wellingcamp's deep voice talk about forgiveness and confessing sins of the heart. Her pastor had stated that only when you confess the guilt from your sin, it detaches from the heart and you are free.

"I can't go back, I am the fornicator," Candace answered the voice.

"When you asked the Lord Jesus to come into your heart, your sins were forgiven. Now, if you have done an offense against one another, you should ask for forgiveness to the one you have offended. If Kareer does not accept your apology, then it is her that will have to deal with the consequences. Your sin has been uncovered, and your heart will be healed," the voice stated as the lights in the elevator turned back on and the elevator returned to the floor where Kareer was sitting.

Damn, thought Kareer as she made eye contact with Candace. She thought that bitch had left. Candace breathed deeply as she began to pray that Kareer would not fight her. Her legs started to shake as she forced her legs to walk to where Kareer was sitting.

Kareer was forced to look at Constance. Scott did have awesome taste. Candace looked like a Norwegian Amazon. Candace had tendrils of blonde hair, and her skin was a reddish tint, with blue eyes. Kareer guessed her height was 5'10", and she probably weighed 130 pounds. Candace could have had any man she wanted. Why did she have to have Scott? Kareer thought.

The silence was deafening between the two women as the wife and the mistress came face to face. Candace had remembered what Pastor Wellingcamp had stated about forgiveness. In order for Candace to break free of her sin and be loosed from it, she had to fast, acknowledge her disobedience and ask for forgiveness from the person she offended.

Kareer dried her eyes and stared at Candace in the face. Candace kneeled on the floor and faced Kareer. She looked up into her eyes.

"I don't know why you called me, but I thank you," Candace stated quietly, unable to look her lover's wife in the eyes.

Kareer was amazed at the boldness of this woman. Kareer's blood was boiling inside as she imagined Scott and this woman stealing intimate moments that were reserved for a husband and wife.

Candace saw the hatred and hurt in Kareer's eyes. Candace wanted to run, but Candace had to have this conversation to be free and healed. If Candace refused the will of God, she would never be able to do the work God had planned for her.

"I know you don't want to hear this right now, but I am truly sorry for coming in-between your marriage," Candace replied.

Kareer clapped. "You are absolutely correct. I don't...you have seen your man, leave me," Kareer spat. This woman had taken the best years of Kareer's marriage and life. Kareer did not want to mourn her husband's death with this witch.

Candace turned to walk away but realized Kareer had no one. There should have been a room full of people, instead she was alone by herself. Oh God, thought Candace as she left Kareer sitting in the chair. Candace went to purchase coffee for herself and mint tea for Kareer. She remembered Scott always talked about how Kareer would drink mint tea to calm her nerves. Ironically, Candace knew more about Kareer than most; in a weird way, they were family.

Kareer heard the familiar heels click on the hospital floor.

"Why are you still here? Go home, let me mourn for my husband by myself," Kareer retorted.

"I want to be anyplace but here. I brought you mint tea. It will calm you. I can't leave you like this. God won't let me," Candace stated as she placed the tea in Kareer's hand and sat beside her.

Kareer reluctantly took the tea from Candace. Kareer eyed the mint tea suspiciously.

"Don't worry; there is no poison…I thought about killing you…but you gave me the greatest gift of all, meeting Jesus Christ," Candace humorously replied.

Kareer crinkled her forehead and stared at Candace for the first time. Kareer thought this woman must be crazy.

"Scott never told me you were delusional, just a home wrecker," Kareer said as the nurse came in with Scott's personal items. She also explained that Scott was being moved to the morgue until the funeral home came to pick him up.

After the nurse left, Candace answered Kareer.

"I deserved that. But in my twisted head at the time, Scott had been mine first. I did not see myself as a home wrecker. Before you got pregnant, Scott and I were engaged. He left me when I was diagnosed with cervical cancer. He did not realize it was detected early and I was cured." Candace stopped. Kareer grimaced; she did not want to hear any anecdotes about Scott and his lover.

"He was always in search of perfection and creating situations that he ran away from, like today." Candace laughed.

Kareer tried to maintain her bitterness, but Candace was warm, charismatic, and honest. Kareer needed another adult to help her cope with all the drama Scott had left her with. Kareer had to agree with Candace, Scott was an escape artist.

"If you are waiting for me to forgive you, it will never happen. How can you say you met Jesus when you were sleeping with my husband, a married man? You destroyed my lovetude," Kareer mouthed.

"I did not expect you to forgive me tonight," Candace replied as she stood up from the seat she was sitting in. Candace kneeled down in front of Kareer's chair and looked up at Kareer.

"When Scott married you, I moved to London to get away from him. I wanted the love of my life to be happy. Even if it was not with me. I stayed in London for five years, but when my company folded, I came back to the states and ran into Scott. I could not stop seeing Scott. It was so natural. I did not care that he had a wife, I needed and wanted him," Candace said.

Kareer wiggled in her seat. She did not want to hear this, and Candace grabbed her hands tighter.

"But then one day I saw a note you put in Scott's pocket. It was a scripture that said, 'I can do all things through Christ, which strengthen me.' Then periodically there were other notes, like 'I love you because God is Love'. I was intrigued. I even started attending your church. I admit, I was curious to see who had my man married, so I guess I was stalking you. As I started attending your church, I became transformed by the renewing of my mind. Jesus came into my life. I had been fighting this temptation to be with your husband. I know I was wrong, and I apologize. I must confess, please forgive me for wrecking your marriage. And I pray that God gives you your attitude of love back. For I know that God is a restorer. Please, dear Jesus, heal Kareer's heart. Restore her faith in love, and give Kareer the love that she needs," Candace prayed as she poured her heart into praying for Kareer.

As Candace prayed for Kareer, all the anger, frustration, hurt, despair, isolation, and loneliness of two broken women were healed through one woman's forgiveness and the other's confession of sin. An unlikely friendship of sisterhood and Christendom was born.

Present

Kareer was awakened by the flight attendant.

"Good evening, ma'am, we are in New York." Kareer smiled as she retrieved her laptop bag.

"Hi, Kareer. It's me, Candace...just called to let you know I'm okay and my husband stated the kids are fine. This trip will change your life forever. When love appears, risk it!" Candace urged.

"Candace, you are always taking care of me!! How are you?" Kareer asked as she saw the driver.

"You know God has me. It was just awful; I hope you can get to the bottom of this. I used DrugCo products all the time," Candace stated.

"I hope so, too," Kareer stated as she said goodbye to her best friend.

The unfriendly driver took her bags and whisked her away into traffic. They arrived at the biggest drug company in the world.

"Well, well, if it isn't the dragon lady herself!" shouted Carlton Buchannan.

Kareer smiled as she hugged her boss.

She played with her brown curls and applied a fresh coat of make-up. She knew she had to look confident and glamorous before talking to the reporters.

She nodded to Buchanan that the company was ready to make a statement. It was her job to convince America that DrugCo could still be trusted.

"Good morning, America, our hearts go out to the families of this terrible ordeal. We are doing everything in our power to assist the authorities to find the solution to the disfigurement of 50 patients. We have compiled a detailed investigation and are cooperating with authorities. I can assure you that all of DrugCo merchandise is completely safe. The plants have been closed where the allegations were made, and we have conducted a thorough investigation. To show our solidarity to the victims of this heinous crime, we will pay all medical costs," Kareer stated with compassion in her voice.

Her voice wavered as she felt faint when she saw him standing in the middle of the room. It had been as if time had transported her back to her freshmen days at the University of La Verne. He was two years older than her, it was love at first sight.

She was jolted back to reality by the reporter stating, "Then your company is liable for the face disfigurement of the consumers?" the reporter stated.

Kareer flashed a winning, movie star smile. "No, we believe in our product. We love our customers. We have been in business for over eighty years. We stand behind our product. We hurt when our consumers hurt, we cry when our consumers are in pain. Anything we can do to help our consumers heal, we will. Without our customers, we don't exist."

He watched her sashay across the stage. He wanted to approach her. He did not know what to say.

"Wow, as always, you are the best" Buchanan stated as he watched the interview from the teleprompter.

"You should have been an actress." He stared at Kareer for the first time. She was a beautiful African American woman.

"Where are you staying?" asked a familiar voice behind her. He was so close to her, she smelled the peppermint on his breath. She was frozen. She did not know what to say. Her heart began to beat rapidly, and her legs became weak. Her eyes darted across the room, looking for refuge. It had been twenty-three years; why should she feel like a young schoolgirl?

Kareer took a deep breath and slowly turned to face the love of her life.

"I thought you were going to let me just stare at your assets all night." He smiled confidently. "Wow, you are still my gorgeous chocolate bar." He could have kicked himself for that. He always seemed to put his foot in his mouth when it came to her. She always seemed to make him uneasy.

"And you are my Irish Oreo cookie," she stated as she regained her composure. She remembered the long walks, the laughter as they drove her little blue Ford Festiva to Vegas when they were students at the University of La Verne.

Their eyes locked as the burning in their hearts began to erupt into an uncontrollable passion; he wanted to pull her into him and kiss her passionately.

She began to breathe faster as she eyed him up and down like a big piece of red velvet cake. She felt her cheeks warm as she remembered the passion between them.

"Hello, Derrick McGraw, it's been a long time. You look distinguished. You look great!" she stated as she let her eyes dance over his chiseled body.

He watched her bedroom sexy eyes. Her eyes could melt a man to his knees.

"Damn, you haven't aged at all," he stated, trying to break the stare. He did not want to sound eager.

Kareer thought of something smart to say. Instead, she swallowed her thought and smiled graciously. Derrick took Kareer by the hand and led her to the corner of the lobby. He stared into her hypnotic eyes.

"Can I take you to dinner? Maybe catch up on old times?" he asked gruffly.

Kareer wanted desperately to say yes. Her heart skipped a beat.

"Okay, I'll meet you at dinner." She had forgotten to ask him where was dinner. She looked at her itinerary.

Kareer was so elated and excited to see Derrick McGraw. Although she could not wait to meet up with him for dinner, she had to create a timeline and a publicity campaign to regain the trust of the public for DrugCo. She had 12 hours before she had to meet with legal and the rest of the publicity team. Kareer had spread all of the information, papers, photos, and case studies on the floor to build a solid publicity campaign. Kareer had been working so diligently, she had forgotten about her dinner date. She heard a light, familiar tap at her hotel room door. Kareer peeped through the peephole and opened the door.

"Are you going to invite me in?" he asked as he waited for the invitation into her room. He wanted to hold her, kiss her, and lay with her. Derrick wanted to know if she had children, if she was married, was she still in love with him.

Kareer was so amazed at how her heart felt, she had forgotten to ask him in. She tried to mouth the words to say sorry for dinner, but she was in a state of shock. How could this be? After 23 years, he had left her speechless. She wanted to ask him if he was married, had children, became a lawyer? Did he ever think about her?

Kareer motioned for him to come in. Derrick obliged.

"Oh, as usual, buried in your work. That's how come you forgot about our date," Derrick stated as he perused her reports.

"What do you do for DrugCo? I saw your name on one of the reports," Kareer blurted out as she watched her ex effortlessly walk towards her; she could not help herself. She missed him dearly. She pulled Derrick into herself and embraced him. She looked up to his 6'2" frame and kissed him passionately. He eagerly returned her kisses. He had to admit, she was never this assertive, he liked this Kareer. Her kisses felt so good, it seemed as if Kareer had always been his medicine. He could not tear himself from the kiss. She smelled good, looked good; he wondered if he took her right now, would she let him?

Kareer pushed him away and tried to regain her composure. His kisses were still delicious. She had never kissed another man like that, not even her husband.

"I'm sorry, I guess I've always wanted to do that," she said as she looked away, embarrassed.

Derrick's eyes laughed as he pulled her into him and kissed her back passionately. This time, he grabbed her and passionately returned the kiss. She closed her eyes and was thankful to be in the arms of the love of her life, basking in the love attitude in the air. After a long embrace, he gently released her.

"I'm glad you kissed me." Derrick replied.

"It's nice to know that you are still attracted to me," he stated breathlessly. She smiled that smile again as they separated. Derrick smiled his million-dollar smile.

"I'm chief legal counsel," Derrick stated.

A lifetime of memories erupted. They both began to talk at once. They smiled at one another.

"Why don't you start?" Derrick stated.

"What would you like me to say?" Kareer asked with a puzzled look her on her face.

There were so many questions she had wanted to ask him. After all this time, how did they end up in the same city, same hotel room, and the same company? She always had a lovetude for Derrick. Derrick was good for her. He taught her how to love, trust, and give. He showed her it was okay to love someone unconditionally. She sighed as Derrick watched her intensely as she paced back and forth in the room, trying to collect her thoughts. She purposely avoided his stare. She did not want him to see the look of confusion on her face. She never could get the love thing right. She thought she had mastered it with her husband, but he disagreed. Her husband blamed all the affairs he had with other women on the fact that she never made him feel like a man.

Kareer thought when she was with Derrick, things were natural. She did not have to force any feelings. Finally, Kareer was tired of pacing, and eventually she sat on the bed. The two lovers stared quietly at each other in their reverie of memories past. Derrick finally broke the silence and talked about the last twenty-three years of his life.

Derrick explained after his graduation he went into the military as an officer and saw action in Desert Storm and Iraq. He wanted to come back for Kareer's graduation and ask for her hand in marriage. The week before his permit to come back to the states was final, his unit was ambushed and he was injured badly. Derrick lost his memory for two years. He returned to the tree four years later, hoping Kareer was still around. He asked everyone in La Verne and Pomona, California, if they had seen her. Some of her friends told Derrick she had left and moved to San Francisco. Derrick missed her. Derrick said that he had wrote a letter to an old address detailing the events of his life, but Kareer had never returned with his answer, and Derrick stated he moved on, married and divorced twice, with four children as well.

Derrick watched her intensely as she remembered that painful year without Derrick. She smiled as she relayed the past twenty-three years back to Derrick.

"I waited six months after I graduated, hoping that you would come back. I took a job at the college as a resident dorm manager. I went to our tree every day at the same time, hoping you would return. I mailed letters to your home, but they were returned unopened. I started dating a man. Six months into the affair, I found out I was pregnant and was going to get an abortion. He told me he would marry me, but he did not love me. I agreed, I did not want to kill my baby, which in turn happened to be fraternal twins." She sighed.

Derrick looked away. He was sad. He had hoped Kareer was single. As he listened more to her story, he could tell that her husband was a jerk. He realized Kareer would never be his.

Kareer continued her story. "About six years ago, Scott, my husband, died from prostate cancer. "I've been alone with the kids since. He had many affairs on me, but now I'm in a much happier place. I forgave him and his mistress. Ironically his mistress is now my best friend, bestselling author of Lovetude and married to a pastor." Kareer half smiled as she watched Derrick's body language.

Derrick eyes grew wide. "Lovetude, should have known her book, our love, nice."

Derrick was elated that Kareer was still single. Both friends continued to talk the night away. They discussed their lives. Both lover friends laughed at the fact they had worked for the last five years in the same company and had never run into one another.

Both friends embraced once again as the euphoria of love overtook their feelings.

"Kareer, I never stopped loving you. I want you in my life," Derrick whispered. He felt he would never let her go. He would wait and fight for her. She was the one. She had always been the one. Kareer had taught him how to be a man. She had taught him how to have an attitude of love.

Kareer wanted to sing at the top of her lungs. Could it be possible in a week to fall back in love with the love of her life?

"Derrick, you do not know how long I've waited to hear you say those words," she whispered as she kissed his soft, sweet lips. She hugged him as all the coldness of her heart melted. Scott had turned her into a hateful old woman. Being with Derrick erased all the pain and despair Scott had caused over the years. Scott had made her forget about the Lovetude she used to have when she was with Derrick. She was so elated Derrick was once again in her life and opened her heart to the possibility of love again.

Kareer looked out the window. It had been hours since they had talked. She looked at the time and realized in two hours she would be meeting with legal, so she had to get some rest. They excused each other and promised after the meeting in the morning they would meet for breakfast. They hugged, and Derrick went back to his room with a school boy grin on his face.

Buchanan came in and called the meeting to order. They went over their action plan and next appointment dates. Kareer watched the room. Buchanan looked tired and nervous. He informed the staff that if they did not handle this situation, they all would be out of a job and may face criminal charges and countless lawsuits from customers. Kareer understood the importance of the matter, however all she could think of was being in Derrick's arms. She wanted to make love and wake up in his arms.

Kareer drowned out Buchannan's voice as she stared directly at Derrick. He was still wickedly handsome. He had long eyelashes, thick, black curly hair, and a baseball body with bulging muscles. Derrick caught Kareer staring at him. He gave her his million-dollar smile, sat back in his chair, and mouthed, "Come and get me, baby." Kareer looked away, embarrassed, hoping no one else saw the lovers dance between Derrick and herself. She smiled as she reminisced about her first encounter with Derrick.

Past

Kareer looked at her childhood room one last time. She was scared and confused. Her mother had told her she would do fine at college, this was it, she was now a woman. Kareer threw the last of her things in her Ford Festiva. Her neighborhood friends bid her farewell as she drove off to a different city and a new way of life.

Kareer had begged her mother to come and participate in orientation with her. Her mother refused, and Kareer was by herself. Everyone else had come with their parents. She stayed in her car for about 30 minutes before she gained the courage to go to her room.

"Hey Derrick, here come the fresh meat!! We even got one from the L.B.C., you know, Long Beach Cali. You know what they say, 'bout Long Beach girls," yelled a big, husky looking guy.

"Really? What they say?" Derrick asked blankly as he was taken aback by the young lady exiting the blue little Ford car that looked like a box. She looked lost. He wondered if she was somebody's girlfriend or sister.

Kareer reminded herself to look straight down as she passed all of the whistles and whispers as she heard them talk about her hair and her clothes that were outdated. She even overheard one of them saying, "Look at the hood rat that was accepted into our school." Another one stated, "Yep, there goes the neighborhood." Kareer knew they were talking about her. To keep the crowd from seeing her disappointment and fear, she focused on the door of the dorm hall and tried to walk quickly. She was three-quarters there when her luggage handle and the bottom support of her luggage fell in pieces on the ground. The group of upper classmen and women laughed as Kareer tried to pick up her things and regain her composure.

Derrick watched as the young lady was heckled as she tried to get the clothes that were now on the lawn of the campus and the girls were holding up her clothes and yelling, "Yard sale." Kareer balled up her fist and was ready to knock some girls out when a young man handed her a trash bag and began to shoo the girls and guys away and helped her pick up her things.

"Thank you," Kareer shyly whispered. Kareer was too embarrassed to look her hero in the face.

"They didn't mean anything by it. Someone always get picked on the first day fresh meat move in. Just glad I could rescue you," he stated as he disappeared and gave her a wink. Kareer finally finished picking up her stuff and made it to her room. She wished she would have stayed in Long Beach; this school was going to be difficult. Kareer put her things away and prepared for a shower. She opened her door, and on the floor of her doorway was a sign that read, "Yard sale, go home, your kind not welcome here." Kareer picked up the sign and hung it on her door. When she made time, she would decorate it and leave it on her door for the whole semester.

Kareer's freshmen orientation commenced. She was the only Black American in the entire group. She wished she had gone to a Historically Black College or University, but this small liberal arts college had given her a full ride. She heard the white girls in the back snicker at her because she looked different. Most of the people were grouped together. She watched as the team leader made his way to the stage. Kareer thought he was the most gorgeous creature on the face of the Earth. She smiled to herself, for he had rescued her yesterday from embarrassment when he helped her pick up her things. He had black curly hair, hazel eyes and nice abs. His teeth were straight, and his voice was melodic and inviting. Kareer had a vivid imagination. He was an upperclassman, he would never notice an African American teen from Long Beach, California.

He made eye contact with a beautiful young lady. He could not understand why she did not have an entourage around her. She was different, and the only African American in the crowd. Derrick McGraw remembered when he was a freshman in college and no one from his hometown had joined him. He understood how she must have felt. The difference between Kareer and Derrick was he was white and wealthy. Derrick had been watching her the whole week. She was all alone. He was going to get her to talk today in the group.

The girls in the back of the room were whispering about her hair and the attire she had on. Some girls could be very mean. Kareer decided that she would graduate at the top of her class.

Derrick tried to act as though he did not know her name when he called on her. He explained each person called upon had to create one word from the two words given. Define it and use it in a sentence.

"First individual we will call upon is Kareer Williams." He smiled, as though pretending not to see her.

Kareer was in a reverie, and she did not hear Derrick McGraw call her name. The girls in the background stop snickering as he called her name twice. Derrick was in a shock. No one had ever ignored him. She made him walk up to her. Kareer was shocked, Derrick was behind her chair. The energy he gave off was overwhelming. He had startled her. Thankful she was milk chocolate color; he could not see that she was blushing. She was day dreaming of him kissing her.

"Ms. Williams your word is love and attitude." Kareer gave him a smile. Kareer was a wordsmith. She was gifted with words, and presentation... She looked up and made eye contact with Derrick. She took the index card and sashayed up to the white board in the room. She wrote in big, sprawling letters LOVETUDE.

The rich girls stop snickering. The whole room became quiet. This was her moment to tell everyone what Lovetude meant.

Derrick was amazed. She was not just a pretty face. One of the rich girls was interested in what it meant and yelled, "Definition, please."

"Lovetude is an attitude of love. The ability to put someone's needs and wants before your own. Igniting an electrifying heat that develops into an inferno of passion that will never be extinguished. A fire that can only be quenched by the reunion of their souls. Realizing the attitude of love has healed all hurt and creates a love renewing force of life," Kareer ended breathlessly.

The entire room of freshmen and orientation leaders was quiet. In a brief few words, Kareer had mesmerized the room. Everyone was on the edge of their seats, waiting for more. Everyone was engrossed in what this new term entitled Lovetude meant.

Kareer stood in front of the room. All eyes were on her. Kareer stared straight ahead into Derrick's eyes, as if to say, "Baby, that was for you." The crowd burst into a thunderous applause as she sashayed to her seat. Derrick was red in the face. He had no idea she could command a room like that. It took a whole two minutes before he could resume as the instructor. As they were dismissed from the group, one of the rich girls approached Kareer.

"Hi, I'm Amanda. You really believe in love like that?" she asked as her group of friends stayed back and watched her.

"Hello, I'm Kareer, nice to meet you. Yes, I do. However, it will probably never happen for me here because some people feel I don't belong. FYI, tell your friends I'm here to stay and I'm optimistic about love. Better be careful, Amanda, your boyfriend might just want some of my Lovetude." Kareer smiled, not knowing if the conversation was going to lead to more teasing.

Amanda looked down and decided Kareer seemed like a pretty cool person.

"Listen, I want to apologize for us...it's just that we are not used to seeing African Americans like us. I mean, you are not pregnant or loud. You are great. You have inspired me today," Amanda stated as she walked away. Kareer smiled, maybe after all, it was a good idea to come to this university.

"Looks like you have become Ms. Popular," Derrick stated as he came from behind.

"Not really, you just put me on the spot on the right day," Kareer responded, masking the excitement of talking to him.

"Good, it is 'bout time that you noticed. Are you free for dinner? I would like to get to know you better," he stated.

Kareer smiled demurely. "Are you safe? My mother warned me about all the upperclassmen. I mean, me being fresh meat and all," she stated playfully.

"I'll be good the first time," he winked.

Present

Kareer was jolted back to reality. "Penny for your thoughts?" Derrick stated as he got close to her and hugged her from behind. Derrick's touch gave her an electrifying jolt.

"Just remembering you and me," she stated as the meeting had finished.

"Let's go to breakfast," he stated as he steered her to the elevator. He wanted Kareer all to himself. He loved being in her presence.

"Excuse me, Kareer, I was wondering if we can get together later?" a man named Tony Lincoln stated.

Derrick gave Tony a rude look. Kareer smiled, as she wanted to accept Tony's offer; after all, she had not even considered other men for the last six years. Kareer was about to say okay when Derrick interrupted Tony.

"Look, Tony, me and Kareer go way back, and we are catching up on old times. I am not afraid to profess my love for this woman. She is the love of my life, and I don't care how long it takes. I want our attitude of love back. I miss our LOVETUDE."

Kareer smiled as Derrick told this stranger he still loved her. They decided to eat breakfast at the Empire State Building.

"Derrick, breakfast here?" Kareer asked. When Derrick and Kareer started dating, he asked her where would she like to visit on their first trip together; she stated the Empire State Building, and there was no way he could have remembered that.

"Because the love of my life stated she had never been to New York and would love to go to the Empire State Building." He smiled. Kareer's eyes twinkled at the thought he had remembered.

"Oh, you thought I forgot?" Derrick stated as his eyes locked in on Kareer and he leaned over and caressed her arms with his hands.

"Baby, I remember everything about you. Your smile, your tenacity...your determination, how you work the room, and most importantly how you make me still feel. I need you. I want you in my life. I'm unattached, I will wait for you. I want you to be my wife. I have to do this now. It's been too long, and we have wasted too much time," Derrick stated gruffly as he looked into Kareer's eyes.

A part of her wanted to believe Derrick. She had heard those words before, and it yielded her a loveless marriage with incredible children. What if he was just saying those things?

Kareer's eyes softened as Derrick caressed her hands and melted the ice that had formed around her heart. What more did Kareer had to lose? Nothing? She would allow Derrick in her heart once more.

Kareer smiled as she stated, "Derrick, I've always wanted you from the moment you took my breath away. I created Lovetude for you. You are my man, my heart, and soul. I love you."

FAMILYTUDE

Familytude

Prologue

Devon smiled as the wind brushed against her cheek. She loved riding in the back seat of the 1988 Wagoner. Devon's parents were arguing over the missed exit of the freeway. Devon's siblings yelled, "FAMILYTUDE!" Familytude was their code word for ceasing arguments. Devon's parents stopped bickering and laughed. Her dad exited the freeway to ask for directions at the gas station. Devon was thankful her dad stopped. She needed to use the bathroom and was out of candy. Devon and her big brother Keith were concerned about the Whittier curse. Today was the Whitter curse anniversary.

"We serve Jesus Christ, Christians can't be cursed," Keith proclaimed, as if he had read Devon's thoughts. He could not let his little sisters see the concern in his face. He was scared. Keith Jr. overheard his parents planning final arrangements in case the Whittier curse was real.

"Did you see that?" Vanessa excitedly yelled as she exited the bathroom.

"It was a blast from the sun! I saw a silver beam by the mountains!" Vanessa screamed as she began to cry. Out the corner of her eye, she saw a white figure lurking by the Wagoner.

"Vanessa, what book are you reading? The silver is just a reflection of the sun. Honey, I told you not to stare at the sun in the dessert. You are seeing a mirage," her mother stated as she embraced her young daughter.

"No, Mom, the curse is happening today!" Vanessa shook and stared blankly. Vanessa's mother held her until the seizure subsided.

"It's time to get back on the road. We have to get to Phoenix before nightfall," Her dad stated as he checked the tires. Keith admired his dad.

"Son, what's wrong?" Keith's dad noticed him staring at him.

"I am glad you are my dad," Keith professed.

"Ah, son, thank you," he stated as he hugged his son. Keith Sr. wished his family could live forever. He hoped the Whittier curse was a myth. Keith Sr. lost his parents in a tragic car accident when he was seventeen years old.

Keith Sr. was placed in foster care, and he had become angry and depressed. He attempted suicide two times. On his last attempt, he met a young lady named Madeline. She was also an orphan; her parents had died in a fire. She saved Keith Sr. and gave him a reason to live. Together, the young couple created their own family based on agape love. They created an attitude about family, love and support. Their term familytude was born.

Keith Sr. hoped his premonitions were fake. He had heard that one always saw a glimpse of their death before they expired. A cold sweat permeated through his body as he tried to erase the gruesome scene of his death.

The family entered the car and went back to driving. Vanessa saw another bright light on the horizon. She looked over at Keith, who was fast asleep. She wanted desperately to tell her big sister, but Devon was furiously writing something in her diary. Her mom was knitting a sweater. She sighed and prayed feverously.

Keith Jr. was jolted awake by a thunderous noise. He felt his body being ejected from the car. The Wagoneer flew off the freeway. The Wagoneer flipped and tumbled into the canyon, landing on its roof. Devon was in excruciating pain. Her mind felt scrambled. Devon was not sure what had happened. She tried to move her legs, she saw them, but they failed to respond to her commands. Devon panicked, she was paralyzed! Devon opened her mouth to scream, nothing came out of her mouth. Devon stared at her brother's severed torso. She turned her head to avoid the gruesome sight. As Devon looked away, she saw the remains of her sister's skull crumbled like grains of salt in the dirt. Devon closed her eyes and prayed this was an ugly nightmare. This was supposed to be the best day of her life. Instead, the Whittier curse was her reality. She was an orphan, the last of her bloodline. She tried to pry herself free from the wreckage of the mangled truck. Some dumb birthday, thought Devon bitterly as she hummed Happy Birthday to herself.

"Hey, help me!!!!" she yelled loudly. The startled figure stopped. "Why do you want help?" it asked as it bent down beside her.

"Your brother is cut in half, your sister has no face, and the headless bodies of your parents are miles from here. What do you have to live for?" the figure tauntingly stated.

"Are you here to help me or watch me die?" Devon spat as her breathing began to stabilize.

The figure cocked its head to the side to think. It kneeled down beside Devon's trapped body. The figure looked confused, contemplating Devon's request.

Devon burned the memory of the figure in her mind. The figure had illuminating, spider-like tendrils growing from the top of its elongated cylinder body. Devon could not tell if the figure was a man or woman, it did not have any facial features. Devon was not sure if she was losing her mind or dying.

Present

Devon shuddered as she awoke from her sleep. Devon sat up on the side of the bed. She was exhausted but afraid to go back to sleep. Every night, she relived the accident of the awful night that altered her destiny forever.

"Mom!" yelled her sixteen-year-old daughter Chasne.

"Are you, all right?" Chasne asked as she approached Devon's door.

"Yes, why are you up so late?" Devon answered.

"I was talking with Pierre, you yelled, 'Somebody help me…help me, please… my family…I can't reach them…they are going to burn…'" Chasne reiterated with concern in her voice.

"Mom, you need help. You have been having the same nightmare for years. You are going to scare away our family tenants. I don't want to live in this big old house by myself. I love Pierre, Milagros, Alex, Manya, Ashlee, Mona and Gary Jones. You need to heal and forget," Chasne stated as she hugged her mother tightly and fell asleep.

Devon put on her slippers and went downstairs. She heard Mona and Gary in the family room. Devon was afraid to live alone. She had purchase the foreclosed mansion when she was discharged from the Navy. Devon's dream was to own a group home for foster children like herself. Her ex-husband ruined her dream when he was caught molesting one of the foster children. Mona and Gary were Devon's first house tenants. They had multiple tragedies in one year. Mona was diagnosed with ovarian cancer. Gary and Mona lost their business, and their only child died in a school bus accident. Gary spiraled into depression, drugs, and pornography. Devon was Mona's oncology nurse, and they developed a friendship. When Devon had heard of the couple's misfortune, she told them she had a room for rent. Devon's home was a refuge for depression, building families, and teaching forgiveness. Mona saw the agony on Devon's face. Mona wished she could eased the nightmares Devon experienced. Mona wished she could take away Devon's pain.

"Another rough night?" Mona asked sympathetically.

"Yes, did I wake you?" Devon asked, concerned.

"No, we were just conversing with Pierre," Mona stated, trying to change the subject since Devon looked agitated.

Devon sighed as she brewed a cup of peppermint tea. Ashlee, the young medical student, came bursting through the door.

"So, did your team finish the cadaver?" Devon asked, trying to forget the nightmare.

"Yes, I have to decide what fellowship I should apply for. My parents want me to return home, but I want to stay here," Ashlee revealed.

"Ashlee, you are always welcome here. However, Dr. Howe believes the best fellowship for you will be in Boston," Devon stated.

"I learned what it means to have a family in this house. If it were not for you and your strong sense of familytude, I would not be graduating summa cum laude," Ashlee compassionately stated.

"Ah, Ashlee, applause…you bring tears to my eyes," stated Alex as he entered the busy kitchen. "Didn't know we were having a family Pow Wow," he joked as he pulled up a chair from the breakfast nook.

"You are jealous because you will no longer have a midnight kitchen raid buddy," joked Ashlee.

Alex was a famous architect. He met Devon in New York. Alex abhorred family because his biological parents abandoned him. Devon's home had become his place of healing from rejection, isolation and allowed him to forgive his parents. Devon smiled at the family banter.

"Mom, Keith sent me a text. He says he wants to find his father," Chasne announced as she came down the stairs. She could not sleep with all the chatter in the kitchen. Devon winced at Chasne's announcement. When Devon was in Iraq, her division was ambushed. Devon was a prisoner of war and raped. After Devon's rescue, her physical revealed she was pregnant. The Navy physician wanted her to have an abortion, Devon refused. Devon's child was the only family she had. She would not kill her child; he was a part of her. She named him after her deceased father and brother, Keith. Devon was determined to continue the legacy of Familytude.

Alex saw the look of pain on Devon's face. Alex texted Keith to schedule a lunch meeting tomorrow. Alex wanted to persuade Keith to stop searching for his past. Alex felt Keith's past could bring ghosts that could harm his future.

Lunch

Alex waited patiently in the lobby of the resident hall at San Francisco University. Alex thought of Keith as the son he never had.

"Hey, Alex." Keith smiled as he embraced the only male father figure he had known. Keith looked up to Alex.

"Wow, Keith!! You look like a Greek god! Amazing how things have changed," Alex joked as they walked to his red Lexus IS250c.

"I'm trying out for the NFL, don't tell my mother. You know how she hates contact sports," Keith boasted as he flexed his protruding muscles. Alex smiled, he remembered when he had those same aspirations. Most little boys dreamed of growing up to play professional sports.

"Damn, Alex, when are you going to get a real car that shows you are a billionaire?" Keith paused. "I mean, if I had your money, I would flaunt it," Keith stated.

"People who pretend, show what they think they have. The real billionaires never show and tell," Alex laughed. Keith nodded and scanned the iPod for music. Keith knew why Alex wanted to have lunch. His big-mouthed little sister Chasne could not keep a secret.

"Why do you need to find this man that violated your mother?" Alex blurted out as the Chinese waitress led them to their seats.

"Haven't you ever wanted to know about your family history?" Keith asked.

Alex took a moment and stared into Keith's green eyes, which was rare for an African American male. Keith's skin was the color of a Snicker's bar.

"No, sometimes the past can tear a family apart?" Alex stated as he looked away, masking the hurt he felt from his own family.

"It's better to forget the past," Alex said.

Keith knew Alex was harboring family wounds. Alex never talked about his past.

"How would you feel if you were a product of rape? It's because of me she's afraid to be in a relationship," Keith angrily stated as he banged his fist on the table.

Alex sympathized with Keith. He never realized the isolation and rejection Keith felt.

"Keith, your mother loves you with all her heart, you are not to blame for someone else's vulgarity," Alex replied adamantly.

Keith paused. "For the past year, I have been searching for my father."

Alex breathed uneasily. He wanted to support Keith, but he had allegiance to Devon. Keith's confession made Alex reminisce about his own family. His biological parents were wealthy. Alex's pediatrician told his parents he would be developmentally delayed. Alex was diagnosed with dyslexia. He was sent to live with his poor relatives. His relatives treated him like an outcast. Alex wanted his family to love him. Alex needed the validation of a family life. Alex reflected back on the words of Keith. If his parents had accepted him, embraced his differences, he would not be a broken soul, afraid to love. Alex was determined to make his biological family accept him. He won a full scholarship to Duke University and graduated at the top of his class. After Alex graduated from college, he went to his parents' home and presented his degree. His parents treated him like a stranger. Alex told them, "You are my parents, but you will never be my family. You are supposed to love me unconditionally. But after today, you are dead to me!" Alex blinked his eyes hard. He wished he had a mother like Devon; she gave one hundred and ten percent in love.

"Your mother chose you. You will break her heart," Alex whispered.

"I know, but I have to heal and forgive. What good will it do me if I'm angry because this man violated my mother? I want him to stare me in my face and see that I am a part of him. Maybe find answers...I don't know, hopefully give my mom a peace of mind," Keith rationalized. Alex's heart ached for Keith.

"What are you going to do when you find him?" Alex asked as his piercing blue eyes stared at Keith.

Keith looked away. He did not have an answer for him. Alex knew that Keith was lying. Keith was stubborn; when he had an idea, he was going to accomplish his goal.

"When are you going to meet him?" asked Alex. Keith did not have the heart to tell Alex he had already met with him and had taken a DNA test.

"He's coming to the Spring Fling at church tonight," Keith whispered quietly.

"I hope things go well for you," Alex stated as the two men ate in silence.

Spring Fling

Chasne was excited about the Spring Fling. The youth of the church organized a yearly spring celebration. This year, Chasne had been elected As the program chairperson. Keith was the first to arrive at the Spring Fling. He was anxiously waiting for his mother and sister. Chasne had rambled on for eight months about the Spring Fling. Keith was impressed. Chasne had thought of everything. The theme of the carnival was titled "Family Affair". He smiled as he thought her theme was fitting.

Tonight, Keith would reunite his mother with her friend, and his father, Isaac Patterson.

Devon was apprehensive because Manya, the youth pastor, told her the guest speaker was from the Middle East. Devon tried to blow it off. The odds were a million to one that he could be her rapist. Devon forced herself to forget about the conversation with Manya and focus on her daughter's happiness. Devon smiled as she pulled into the parking lot. The church was packed with families and friends having a great time. Chasne had carnival rides, food booths, and entertainment and resource tables. Her breath stopped as she stared into the eyes of her rapist. Devon was horrified. He was walking and laughing with Pastor Adams. Pastor Adams saw Devon and walked over to her.

"Devon, I want you to meet a good friend of mine. He is the pastor from our Dubai ministry."

Devon could not control her emotions; she spat in his face.

"He might be your friend, but he is nothing to me," Devon growled.

Pastor Adams was shocked. Abdul looked away as he remembered the American he rescued. She had been beaten and violated. She was a wounded animal with a broken spirit.

Abdul raised his head and stared directly into her eyes as he reassured Pastor Adams.

"The pain never stops until you forgive," Abdul stated in perfect English.

"May God bless you, Devon. Ask God to heal your heart, so you can forgive and love. I think you have the wrong perception of me," Abdul stated quietly.

Devon never lost her cool, but this time his words hit home. She remembered his rough hands and husky, growling voice. She remembered him on top of her as she fought for her virginity.

"I am so sorry, Abdul," Pastor Adams apologized as he gave Abdul his handkerchief.

Abdul raised his head and stared directly into her eyes as he wiped the saliva from his face.

"Pain never stops until you forgive," he whispered again.

Alex arrived as the commotion from the altercation dissipated. Standing beside Keith was a man with a striking resemblance to Keith. Alex was confused, no wonder Keith had been sure Isaac Patterson was his father. Keith looked similar to Isaac.

"You are the worst kind of manipulator. I ought to kill you for raping Devon!" Alex shouted.

Isaac looked perplexed. Isaac obliged when Keith asked him to take a paternity test. Isaac knew the results would exclude him from the test. He was Devon's superior officer and five years older than her. Devon was a child. He would have never abused his position. The results revealed Isaac Patterson was the biological father of Keith. Isaac was shocked because he never had sex with Devon.

The results were a blessing in disguise. Isaac had always wanted a family, but due to his injury in Iraq, he was sterile. His wife divorced him because Isaac could not father children. After his divorce, Isaac became bitter. He needed a family to validate his reason for life.

The bell ranged to announce church service. Manya spotted Chasne and motioned for her to come to the pastor's study.

"I don't want your mother here. Abdul is going to preach the Gospel," Manya whispered.

"I will not leave. I am going to stare that monster in the face. I am going to make him feel the pain he caused me," Devon stated as she washed her face. She was ready to face the demon of her past.

Abdul saw Devon as she entered the church. Devon noticed Abdul staring at her as she glared back at him.

"Praise the Lord, Saints!!!" Abdul stated as he preached from the book of Acts.

"Forgiveness is granted by Jesus Christ. We must forgive if we want to inherit eternal life. Those who refuse to forget the past may turn into a pillar of salt, like Lot's wife did. What will you forget and forgive to move on with your life?" Abdul stated slowly as his eyes pierced Devon's soul. Abdul made Devon cry, she began to remember the events of that awful night.

"I am a filthy rag. It was the favor of God that allowed me refuge and redemption after Iraq. I found Christ in the military, I am now a general in God's Army," Abdul stated as he walked over to Devon.

Devon tuned out Abdul as the memories of her past were revealed.

Past

Devon awoke to the figureless shape in front of her. The figure looked shocked and disappointed. Devon was mad and wanted to go home. She was in pain.

"Am I destined to keep seeing these tragedies?" Devon screamed at the figure. The figure looked angry.

"Stop looking, come help me. I don't want to die." Devon began to sob.

The figureless shape inched closer and touched Devon's belly. The figure shook uncontrollably as it scanned her memory of the explosion.

Devon was no longer scared of the thing that she met years earlier.

"You stare…you look at me like a piece of meat…eat me!!! You won't help me! You look at me as if I make you sick. Be gone, ugly figure." The faceless figure made Devon so mad, she wanted to kill the thing that had tormented her for years. In her rage, she hadn't noticed the figure made a hole to hide her from the enemy. There was a sharp pain in her womb. Devon thought she must have fallen harder than she thought from the bomb attack. She felt herself being pulled up to the sky. She looked below her feet and saw the ground quickly disappear as her body rapidly approached a slender looking white tower in the sky. She heard screams of agony inside the cylinder. Devon was disoriented. It smelled like rotten eggs and burnt wood. Her body stopped floating and fell on a stone table. A three-foot creature approached her, raised her buttocks up and inserted a cold metal substance inside her vagina. She felt as if her entire reproduction system was on fire and reeked of seared flesh.

Devon awoke in a dark room. She heard the Iraqi discussing something. She tried to raise herself up, but the pain between her legs was unbearable. She touched the side of her thigh and felt blood. She tried to stand up, but the force was too heavy, her body went limp and she fell on the dirt floor. Tears escaped her eyes as she tried to remember the events of the last 24 hours. The Iraqi with the beady little eyes peered in and brought her water. Her vision was blurred, and she could not see all of him. He came closer and gave her a dusty cup with a strange liquid in it.

"Here… you…take it help you," he urged in broken English. She remembered his voice yelling to be quiet. She remembered him putting his large, rugged hands over her mouth and his body on top of her. Devon began to shake uncontrollably as she realized this tall Iraqi had violated her. She threw the cup at him and huddled in the corner. He walked over to her and wrestled with her. Devon fought back with all the strength she had. She was not going to let the enemy hit her again. Abdul looked around for something to knock her out. They would hear her. He had to calm her down if he was going to rescue her. Abdul prayed, "Jesus, forgive me," as he picked up a rock and knocked her out.

Devon remembered everything!!!! Abdul did not rape her! He rescued her. Devon stood up in front of the congregation and without containing herself yelled, "Pastor Abdul, forgive me!!!! I thought you raped me. Abdul, you saved my life. Will you accept my apology?" Devon cried.

Keith looked at Isaac. Keith balled up his fist, ready to strike, when a huge, glowing white cloud appeared in the ceiling of the church.

The grayish figure looked directly at Keith and spoke without moving its mouth. Keith rubbed his eyes.

"Isaac did not rape your mother. Evil beings abducted your mother and Isaac. Your mother was artificially inseminated with Isaac's sperm. You are not a product of rape. It was a test. Your mother chose life, you, she fought for a family when her bloodline was eradicated. Devon created a family from strangers, and because of her kindness and forgiveness, the Whittier curse is no more. You are healed. Your future generations will always be blessed. Forgiveness and family love is the key. I will always be there for your protection." The figure disappeared. Keith was at peace as he made his way to his mother and father Isaac. The three adults looked at one another and embraced.

"Devon, I can't explain this. It is unbelievable," Isaac stammered. The bitterness melted from Isaac heart. Isaac felt invigorated. He had a son!

"Thank you for healing my heart, Keith! I'll help mend the broken pieces of our relationship. I will continue the legacy of Familytude," Isaac replied. He was happy to be blessed with a family, and his faith in God was restored.

MARRYTUDE

Marrytude

Deena smiled as she looked over the course of her life. It had been difficult to arrive at this moment, but she thanked God she was happy, no longer afraid of the success God had for her. She looked at her cell phone as she read the text. The text stated, one hour till we meet for our secret rendezvous.

Deena smiled as she cleared off her desk. Sometimes she wondered if she had made the right decision to embark upon the journey as a business owner, lover, wife, child of God. Deena was thankful for her husband Aidan. He lifted her up and taught her many things. He showed her what it was like to have a husband led by God. Deena put her wig on her head and dark glasses. The rule was no one could see her, it would destroy her husband's growing architecture firm and the marriage ministry at church. They had been married for fourteen years, and on the verge of divorce twice. Deena was once a single mother to their oldest child, but God changed Aidan's heart and confirmed that Deena was the wife God had for him. She sighed, grabbed her keys to the Range Rover and locked her office door. She really had to stop making these afternoon dates. People, especially church people, would not understand the need for sexual freedom, thirst for adventure, excitement, and fear of being caught. In those two hours with her lover, she was rejuvenated, and infused with energy to deal with the complexities of life.

"Hi, honey," Deena stated as she answered her cell phone.

Aidan loved his wife's voice. She sounded like an angel.

"I just called to say I love you," he sang through the phone. Deena's face glowed as she heard her husband's voice. Every time she heard him, her heart burned with desire. The thought of his touch, him inside her, made her insides salivate at the union of the two married souls.

"Don't forget to pick up the strawberries and cream for tonight's ministry meeting." Aiden stated as he mentally checked off the refreshments for tonight's marriage lesson. Deena smiled as she clicked the off button on the phone. Her heart raced as she floored the Range Rover to her destination. As she exited the 105 freeway, she noticed she had arrived first at the motel. She grabbed her goody bag and checked to see if her lotion, tickler, and ring were in the bag. Her lover enjoyed toys. He claimed it sparked spontaneity and made their sessions memorable. It was food to get through the rest of the week.

Deena opened the door, went inside and put on her hooker clothes. She placed the tickler feather and lotion on the bed, then she waited patiently for her lover to arrive.

"Pastor Aiden, can I talk to you?" asked his church secretary.

"I'm running late, can it wait?" he asked, walking to his car.

"But Pastor, you normally do not have meetings scheduled for your job. I was wondering if you could have lunch with me? Chase is out philandering again, and I don't know what to do," said his flirtatious church secretary, Constance.

"How about we meet an hour before the marriage ministry and discuss strategy?" Aiden stated as he eyed his watch.

Constance gave him a raised eyebrow as she placed her hands on her hips, licked her lips in a come and get me manner and slowly walked away, defeated. Constance was not giving up that easily. She was going to get Pastor Aiden between the sheets one way or the other. She needed sexual healing, and if her no good husband was cheating, she would make her husband feel her pain. What better way than to do it with the associate pastor of the marriage ministry?

Constance grabbed her purse and decided to follow the pastor. It seemed very strange that every Thursday from 1 to 4pm he had a date or calendar blocked out and would never mention what his appointment consisted of. Today was the day of reckoning, she was going to find out. No one had a perfect marriage, and she was going to reveal to the entire church congregation that Aiden and Deena's marriage was in trouble.

Deena heard the familiar sound of the car as it pulled into the near empty parking lot. Deena excitedly lay on the bed with legs open wide, excitedly anticipating her lover's touch. He arrived looking sexy in a blue track suit. He enjoyed his time with his lover.

"Ah, baby," he stated as he grabbed and kissed her forcefully. Deena's body responded as she pulled her body into his, feeling the protruding member trying to connect with her red bikini underwear.

"Let me look at you," he stated as he broke the embrace and stared at her beautiful face and body.

Deena always seemed to excite him. He wondered what character she would be today. He loved her spontaneity. Deena was an upright woman to the world. Behind the doors and secrecy of their love feast, she was a voracious tiger that kept him wanting all of her. He was falling more in love with her.

Constance had never seen Pastor Aiden fly out of the parking lot. He weaved in and out of traffic. Constance followed in hot pursuit, trying not to lose him. Constance finally watched the car park. She was shocked! No wonder Aiden had turned down her many advances, he had a woman on the side! All kinds of thoughts went through her mind. A part of Constance felt defeated and hurt. What was the point of being a Christian when leaders were faking and having affairs? She felt Pastor Aiden didn't have the decency to hide it. The seedy hotel was ten minutes from church. Constance remembered a sermon he had preached: your sins will find you out.

In Constance's disbelief, she called the only man that understood her. She called her husband. Constance wanted to shout it out to the world that Pastor Aiden was a lying, fake, cheating husband. Her palms were wringing wet as she braced herself to talk to her husband.

As she listened to her husband on the other end of the phone, she hoped he didn't rush her off the phone.

"Yes?" Chase answered. He really did not have time to talk to her, but it was her voice today that made him make time for her. She sounded defeated, tired, and disappointed. Damn, thought Chase, did he leave evidence of his latest lunchtime tryst? He wondered if she had found a phone number, pair of panties, or perfume scent on his clothes.

"Can we have lunch?" Constance was alarmed of what she said. Of all things, she maliciously wanted to expose Pastor Aiden, but instead what spewed out of her mouth was lunch with her husband Chase, the cheater!

Chase raised his eyebrows, lunch for him was hours ago.

"How about a nice, romantic, late dinner after the marriage ministry?" he stated.

For years, Constance had begged, pleaded, and urged her husband to go to the marriage ministry. Lately, Chase had been changing. He started bringing her flowers, dates on the weekend, and lunch time talks.

Even though she wanted to expose Pastor Michaels, what cost was she willing to risk? She had almost lost Chase before due to her gossiping with the other ladies of the church. But this time it was different. She had proof. She decided she would pray about it.

"Well, baby, are we on for a date after marriage ministry?" Chase asked, hoping to find out why Constance had called him in the first place.

Constance reluctantly agreed. She was torn between exposing Pastor Michaels and restoring her marriage. When they first begin counseling over two years ago, Chase's major issue with Constance was her gossiping and refusing to have sex three times a day. Constance's issue with Chase was cheating and not coming home at night. Chase had changed. He came home at night, and Constance learned how to cook, clean and satisfy her husband in bed. They had taken the advice of Pastor Michaels and Deena and dated each other...Chase was not convinced. He felt it in his soul something was eating at his wife. He prayed the gossiping had not started again. If she broke their agreement, then he would file for divorce. He loved Constance, but there was only so much he could deal with. Her gossiping ruined a marriage, and produced a suicide in the church that harmed the pastor's family. Chase gave Constance an ultimatum, stop gossiping, or their marriage was over.

Constance sat in the parking lot and watched Deena pull up. She was a nice woman, and very compassionate. Even though Deena had agreed with Chase and believed that a woman should submit to her husband, Constance wondered how she would feel if she found out her husband was cheating.

Constance decided she was going to do some snooping. She was going to hypothetically ask Deena what she would do. Deena smiled as she saw Constance running to her.

"Hi, Sister Deena, how are you?" Constance stated as she grabbed the bag out of Deena's truck. Deena looked at Constance suspiciously. Deena had good discernment about people. Constance was fishing for something. Deena decided to play along.

"I'm good, how are you?" answered Deena.

"I was wondering what should I do if I have proof that someone is a hypocrite in our church?" Constance asked as the two women went to the kitchen of Saint Paul Missionary Baptist Church.

Deena showed a look of frustration at Constance. Constance was constantly in other people's business. Deena thought that this chapter of Constance existence had ended. Deena exhaled in a moment of exasperation, sometimes the hardest addictions to overcome were social. Gossiping was not seen as an addiction, but gossiping destroyed friendships.

"Are you sure?" asked Deena with raised eyebrows. Deena crinkled her forehead, trying to figure out if Constance had somehow uncovered Deena's secret. Deena remembered a quote someone had once stated the truth is encapsulated in a lie. Constance was a gossiper, but her facts were truthful.

The old Constance would have blurted it out. Instead, she decided to wait and pray about her ordeal. A part of Constance wanted every woman to feel the pain of a cheating husband. However, she remembered Chase's ultimatum: one more gossip, and they were through. She sighed as she walked with Deena to the kitchen of St. Paul Missionary Baptist church. The other ladies of the marriage couples' ministry joined in to help prepare dinner. Before the actual marriage session commenced, the ladies were responsible for preparing the meal, and the men were responsible for preparing the room. Pastor Aiden and Deena had set it up that way to mirror how things should work in a marriage.

"Deena. I have to applaud you and Aiden. We have been coming to this ministry for one year, and our marriage gets stronger every year. I just love this. Donald and I come from single parents. We don't know what a real marriage should look like. We did not have examples growing up. All couples need this," Tracy Taylor stated as she praised Deena. The other ladies chimed in agreement.

Constance stood back and watched. She agreed, even her troubled marriage was on the mend. The secret Constance had was tearing her apart. In marriage ministry, there was an open form. She would ask a hypothetical inquiry. Whatever the outcome was, she would follow. Pastor Aiden breezed in as though nothing had happened. Constance was uneasy as the couples discussed how faithful Aiden and Deena were and how they were able to keep their love intact and faithful. Deena noticed Constance's body language and thought about their discussion. Deena wondered if Constance had discovered her secret. Chase watched his wife. She was uncomfortable, oh God, thought Chase. His face fell, Constance was getting ready to run her mouth. He watched her leg as she twirled it around. Chase's piercing blue eyes glared at his wife. Constance saw Chase's stare out of the corner of her eye. She acted like she did not notice. Pastor Aiden always opened with a cute anecdote or sexy flirt quote for his wife. Deena blushed like a school girl.

Constance stared at the floor. She was confused, he was flirting with his wife, winking and sending her kisses across the room, but two hours ago he was in the arms of another woman. Constance felt as though she was betrayed.

For one moment, Constance sympathized with Deena. All the feelings she thought she had overcome with Chase's infidelity came rushing back. She hated Pastor Aiden for being a hypocrite and dishonoring his vows. She hated Chase for having sex with every woman he saw, she hated her deceased father for having sex every Thursday night with the next-door neighbor, while her mother worked double shifts at the hospital.

"Constance, you've been very quiet." The room became very quiet, everyone in the marriage ministry understood what each couple was fighting to survive in their marriage. Each week, Pastor Aiden would pull a topic out of the couples' hat, along with a name for someone to answer. The two issues Constance and Chase were working through were cheating and gossiping.

Constance shook her head. God did have a sense of humor. How would Constance answer? The very thing she had an urge to tell could destroy so many good lives tonight. Chase looked earnestly at his wife. She looked as if she was deep in thought.

"I was trying to remain quiet, so I wouldn't have to answer," Constance joked.

"Everybody knows my story. Five years ago, I would have blurted it out, not caring who I hurt, not consulting Christ for my answer. Today, I am torn. Do I want my best friend to live a lie?" Constance paused as she stared at Deena, as if to tell her subconsciously her husband is a liar and a cheat.

"No, I don't. Would she even believe the words out of my mouth? But scripture tells the truth shall set you free. I would seek wise counsel, have my witnesses ready, and pray. There is strength in numbers. I would tell her... support the married couple because marriage was built to last." Constance thoughtfully said.

Constance smiled as she thanked God for her revelation. She would confront Aiden and Deena. This time, she would do it correctly. She would request a meeting with Pastor Gregory, his wife, Deena and Aiden.

Chase stared at his wife in disbelief. Who was this woman? She looked more beautiful than she had ever been. She looked as if she had transformed into a beautiful, wise woman of God. He smiled. These past three years, she had grown. In the past, the whole city of Downey, California, would have known in 5 minutes about the situation. She was the mouth in the house of Los Angeles County. Deena gave Constance an agreeable smile. Constance now knew what she had to do.

After the meeting, she called and left a message for the senior pastor of the church. Chase smiled lovingly at his wife as he put his arm around her waist.

"Hey, honey, are you ready for dinner?" he stated as he smiled and winked. Constance had so much on her mind, she forgot about the dinner date. She remembered she had food marinating in the refrigerator. Maybe she could satisfy her mate with food at home and a night of marital bliss. That would make Chase ecstatic.

"We could go home." Constance winked in the sexiest whispered voice she could muster. She never knew how to be sexy. Her parents always argued, and she never saw her parents joke or flirt in front of her. Constance had to admit, it was nice how Aiden and Deena showed their affection for one another. It was a shame she had to reveal Pastor Aiden's secret.

Chase smiled as he quickly ushered her to the car. In the car, he watched Constance as she stared ahead at the road.

Chase broke the silence.

"I was proud of you tonight," stated Chase. Constance smiled as she looked at her husband. Her husband was gorgeous. He was 6'2", close cropped brunette hair and chiseled arms and legs. He was an ex-Navy SEAL that kept his body in tip top shape. Chase was ten years older than Constance, but he looked ten years younger.

"Thank you," she stated as she looked away. She turned off her cell phone as she read the confirmation email from Pastor Gregory's wife. She had to find a way to ask Chase to come with her tomorrow. She would after dinner. This time, Constance had proof.

"Oh, I am so amazed and proud how you answered Aiden. Baby, thank you for growing and trying to make us work. I'll have you know that I have turned down thirty women this week," Chase boasted, proud of himself for exhibiting self-control. A year ago, if he saw a beautiful woman, he would have had sex with her. It is a constant struggle, but he thanked God for forgiveness and accountability partners that loved the word of God more.

Chase pulled into the gated community and opened the door for his young trophy wife. After tonight, she was no longer the beautiful, archetype Miss America, she was his lady, lover, wife.

Constance caught Chase's stare. It was a look of love, admiration, she was no longer a trophy wife. Damn, thought Constance, Chase finally fell in love with her, but now she had to tell the truth for her breakthrough.

She opened the door and went to the kitchen to prepare the meal. While she sat at the table, Chase came up behind her and hugged her intimately. She turned around to meet Chase face as he kissed her slowly and tenderly. Constance's heart felt a rush of passion as he picked her up and placed her on the counter and they shared hours of marital bliss. He caressed her soft, supple body as she laid in ecstasy, shaking in the aftermath of their lovemaking. Chase came back with warm towels and her robe to help his beautiful wife clean up.

Constance felt good and. Her husband of eight years had finally made love to her and showed expressions of love.

"Chase, can you come with me tomorrow?" Constance stated, barely above a whisper.

"Yes," Chase stated as he excused himself to the bathroom.

Constance had no other way to tell Chase than to show him the man Aiden Michaels was. She had hired a private investigator. It was not fair to have people believing a lie. She spread the envelope with the pictures all over the bed. She went downstairs and lay prostrate before God. Tonight, was the best night of her life, and probably the last. Constance asked the Lord to make everything all right. It was hard to be a real Christian when everyone was hypocritical.

Chase came out of the bedroom. "Oh, damn," he stated as he saw the all too familiar pictures and brown envelope. Chase was confused. He had been so good lately. He looked closer at the pictures. He was relieved, but he was outraged. He had sung Aiden's praises to all his co-workers, and this man was cheating on his wife. Chase did not know whether to leave Constance for snooping or knock out Aiden for being phony. All Chase's life, he had stayed away from church because of the hypocrisy. And when he had finally embraced the faith, a strong, upstanding black man as a role model, Aiden had fallen.

Chase ran down the stairs to find his wife in tears, lying on her stomach.

She heard Chase's feet as he ran down the stairs. She looked up in defeat. She started playing out the scenarios in her head. She wondered what he would do. He did say if she started gossiping again, they were through. Constance had not told anyone about her investigative tactics. Since the suicide in church, she had learned not to expose it out in the open. Constance knew she could be jeopardizing her marriage, and the marriages of the other couples.

Chase stared at his wife. Constance looked up at her husband in defeat. Chase sat down on the sofa and extended his hands to her. He motioned for Constance to sit beside him.

Chase broke the silence and asked, "Why are you crying?" He felt uncomfortable. He was relieved it was not him this time, but he felt sympathy for his wife. She had grown to love Aiden and had secretly wished that Aiden was her faithful husband. Ironically, Aiden the pastor that had preached fidelity, was messing around on his gorgeous wife. Chase was not attracted to African American women, but Deena was a beautiful, milk chocolate beauty that was supportive, graceful, and kind. Deena kept herself together and had those eyes that would make any man want to bed her. This just proved that men can't be faithful, and his sexcapades were part of the male rites of passage.

"I'll pack my bags. I'll be gone in the morning," Constance replied as she stood up from her seat. Chase grabbed her hand.

"Why are you leaving?" Chase asked, perplexed.

"You told me if I uncovered some more gossip, our marriage is over. I'm tired of the fight. I'm tired of us," Constance stated as she pried her hand from Chase and went up the stairs.

She wished the brown contents of the envelope were Chase's items and she could walk away from her marriage of eight years. Instead, she had messed up again. As a little girl, she remembered how she thought if she kept the house clean, made elaborate meals for her parents, she could stop her father from cheating and her mother from drinking. Constance worked so hard to keep her mother and father happy, but her mother still was a workalcholic and her father kept cheating. Constance sat on the bed and began to cry. She had tried so hard, and things were coming apart. Maybe being single was best for her. Constance began to process her next steps. She wiped her tears away and began to pack her bags.

Chase stood in the doorway as he saw the shadow of his wife.

"Constance, you are not going anywhere. I love you. I'm sorry I have hurt you, Pastor Aiden has hurt you. Baby, I will support you tomorrow, because he lied to all of us, and maybe he'll feel remorseful, I hope so. Maybe in all of this, the marriage ministry can be saved, and maybe marriages can heal the way God wants them to heal," Chase stated as he grabbed his wife and turned her to him.

"I love you with everything in me. No other woman makes me feel the way you do. I know what I said, but that was over three years ago. I understand what my father always professed to my mother," Chase pleaded as he kneeled down on one knee.

"I don't think I ever proposed before. I love you and need you. Damn it, baby, I'm in love with you, and I promise for the rest of my life I will be the husband you need me to be." He had planned to ask her for a recommitment of their vows, but the words erupted out of his mouth like a volcano. She deserved the best, and he was ready now to be the husband God had ordained for her. He pulled out a 15-carat princess cut ring.

Constance could not believe what she saw. She cried as he placed the ring on her finger. Constance was unsure of the outcome of tomorrow, but she embraced her husband lovingly, her heart warmed over.

Constance blinked her eyes and smiled deeply. All Constance ever wanted was to be loved and cherished. She had finally obtained her goal, and now she was going to destroy another marriage with the truth. Ironic how one marriage could flourish, while the other marriage was in shambles. Chase embraced his wife with unrequited love and embraced his wife passionately.

Deena smiled as she ran the bathwater for her and Aiden. The Marrytude session was a breakthrough. Couples were finding their rhythm, and hopefully Aiden would obtain a higher position at St. Paul Missionary Baptist Church.

As Aiden entered the bathroom, he looked worried. "What's wrong? You look worried," asked Deena. "Pastor Gregory wants to meet tomorrow night," Aiden replied with a hint of concern on his face.

Deena looked sympathetically at Aiden. Aiden was ready to take the Marrytude ministry to another level. However, some senior pastors were not ready for the next level. Deena smiled, sometimes church folks were afraid of what God had for them.

Deena embraced her husband, being close to Aiden made her insides jump. She loved her husband deeply. "Aiden, God will work it out. God always does." Deena smiled as she led her husband to the bathtub. They believed in being sensual, kinky, and adventurous in the bedroom. Their attitude about marriage entailed a strong physical attraction, showing each one how they loved one another.

Aiden smiled as he eagerly followed his sexy wife. She slowly undressed him and guided him into the lightly almond scented bubble bath. He smiled as she slowly stood on the bath rug and undressed for him. Damn, thought Aiden, his wife was sexy, beautiful, and wickedly nasty. Her touch made him forget about the nervousness he felt at the bottom of his stomach. He silently prayed that Pastor Gregory would understand his plight.

The look of appreciation on her husband's face should have been enough to calm her fears. Instead, she was apprehensive about the meeting tomorrow. She hoped no one had found out about her secret. Deena stepped into the tub as her husband wrapped his strong arms around her voluptuous body. The closeness they shared was spiritual. The love between a married man and married woman that loved God was ethereal.

"Baby, God, just spoke to me," Aiden whispered as he kissed her on the side of her neck.

"Everything is going to be all right," he said as he made loved to his sexy wife in the beige Jacuzzi bathtub. Deena smiled widely after their lovemaking fest. How could she ever let her man go? She had the best of both worlds. Aiden could hit her spots and give her multiple orgasms. Aiden always put her to sleep.
He brought the towel into the bathroom and scooped up his wife.

"Baby, are you ready for round two?" he playfully stated as he placed her on the bed.

Deena hungrily obliged as they played, embraced and loved one another all night.

Pastor Gregory was angry and hurt. He looked at his watch. He had prayed that Constance had fabricated a huge lie, however pictures do not lie. He was so distraught. He had come to love Aiden like a son. The marriages in the church were thriving. Marrytude, the marriage ministry, was the strongest auxiliary in the church. It would have to be torn down because it was not of God

.

Pastor Gregory looked at Constance and saw the hurt. She no longer revealed hate or contempt. She bore humility and despair on her face. Pastor Gregory looked at Chase, her husband; he looked stooped over and confused. Pastor Gregory was apprehensive. Constance was known as the church gossiper. Constance was the reason Pastor Gregory's son committed suicide in the foyer of the church on Easter Sunday. Pastor had opened testimony Sunday, and Constance came to the front of the church and accused Pastor Gregory of being a hypocrite because he talked against homosexuality in the church, yet his son and lover were eating and sleeping in pastor's house. While Constance exposed the truth, Pastor Gregory's son left his seat and went to the foyer of the church.

He scrawled out big letters on the walls with a thick red permanent maker. "You call yourselves Christians in your fake worship, you profess to love Jesus, honor your word, but how can you say you love Christ, how can you if you don't love me? I am a homosexual, I don't know why I am, and I can't help who I love. I was never raped by a man, my father and mother loved me, never molested by other cousins, I don't want to be a woman. I don't like my life, but how can you say you love Christ, how can you if you don't love me? I am a homosexual. I don't like my life, because I have to pretend, but after today I'm free from all you hypocrites!" He pulled the trigger. The sound of the .45 was rippling. The entire congregation stared in disbelief. Pastor Gregory gripped his heart, First Lady Gregory stared, frozen. Deena rushed into action and raced to the front of the room. Constance watched in awe. Her mouth had caused a young man to take his life. The children were quickly rushed out of the church. The once sacred place to cast all of your troubles had turned into the aftereffects of a war torn, bomb-ridden city. It seemed like hours before the ambulance and police arrived.

Constance's voice returned Pastor Gregory from his reverie.

"Pastor, I know we have been here before. I really wish it was not me. I was not fishing for information. Believe it or not, I was truly minding my own business. I was working on the issues from my heart and marriage," Constance explained as she told the others how she had discovered proof of Aiden's infidelity.

"One day I went to the mall, and I saw Pastor Aiden kissing a lady in a mini dress with sunglasses on and a short haircut. I did not see her face. The next time, I saw him with another classy lady. She was thicker and taller than his wife. So, I hired an investigator. When the pictures came, I decided to follow him and see for myself." Constance stated in despair; in the past, Constance's eyes would have gleamed over, her mouth would have watered to spread true gossip. Pastor Aiden was good for the church and marriages.

"Pastor, I honestly did not want to have to bring this to you at all," Constance stated soberly as she looked at the expressions on their faces. Pastor Gregory looked disappointed and forlorn. Katherine Gregory, wife of Pastor Gregory's, face was frozen in fear. Chase's cheeks were red; his heart was beating fast. Whenever Chase was angry, he wore his feelings on his face.

"Maybe I should just say nothing and leave. I'm afraid I just don't want another incident like five years ago," Constance stated as she rose from her chair. She walked to the door. She placed her hands on the knob as Aiden stared into her eyes. Aiden's heart fell to the bottom of his stomach. His discernment of situations was keen. Deena stopped dead in her tracks as all eyes were on her.

The silence thickened as Aiden walked to the empty chair and sat down. Aiden wondered why Chase and Constance were present. Were they on the brink of divorce? Usually, this meeting was designed for the senior pastor of the church and Aiden to discuss the upcoming three months of Marrytude.

Deena was not as trusting as Aiden. Katherine Gregory kept eyeing Deena in a strange way. Deena was always straightforward. Deena broke the silence.

"Pastor Gregory, are you firing my husband?" She paused. "Oh, I forgot, you cannot fire a volunteer that has degrees in psychology, theology, and a PhD in architectural design." Deena stated, preparing for battle for her husband. Deena calmed down as she looked at her husband. He looked so handsome sitting comfortably in his seat. It was as if the presence of the Holy Spirit was present. No fear was in him. Deena thought maybe that was how Daniel felt in the lion's den. Aiden motioned for Deena to come sit beside him. The corners of his mouth made a brief smile. His wife was elegant, but she could also fight physically and spiritually. She was a jewel for life.

Constance saw the telepathic connection between Aiden and Deena. She frowned at how poor Deena was so

in love with her manipulating husband. Constance wondered if she was blinded like that for Chase.
Pastor Gregory cleared his throat to break the silence.

"Deena, yes, we are here to discuss your husband's fate," Pastor Gregory replied curtly.

"I also hope Aiden will confess his sins and take his chastisement graciously," Pastor Gregory continued.

"No disrespect Pastor Gregory, but get to the point. If you don't want me here, say it, I'll leave," Aiden quietly stated, feeling rejected. He squeezed his wife's hand.

Deena squeezed his hand back and gave him a wink. The wink was reassurance that wherever he was going, she was with him. Chase was a known philanderer. If Pastor Gregory wanted to fire him because of a statement Chase had stated, then St. Paul was not the church for his family.

"Pastor, isn't this enough torture for your family? Constance destroyed the church once, you are going to let her tear it down again based on her half-truths?" Aiden reasoned, still in control.

Pastor Gregory was conflicted. He silently prayed to himself. He was a man of God. He had never cheated on his wife and had never compromised the church.

"Aiden, just confess, we can begin the healing process," Pastor Gregory begged.

"Pastor, I have nothing to confess. The only sin I have done is maybe loving my wife too seductively," Aiden replied as he kissed his wife passionately on the lips. Deena's insides quivered as his lips left hers.

"I've been quiet long enough. You are a devil from the pit of hell. You've been cheating on Deena for over a year," Constance shouted as she threw the pictures at him. Deena glared at him in shock. Before she could control herself, she was on top of Aiden, punching him in the face. In her rage, she knocked him out of his seat on the floor and continued punching him.

The two men grabbed Deena and restrained her. Aiden was dazed and confused.

"When did you have time?" Deena stated, feeling hurt and ashamed that these church folks had to see her act this way.

Aiden ignored Deena. He glared at Constance. "You wanted me that bad, you had me followed?" Aiden mouthed as he took the handkerchief out of his pocket to wipe the blood away from his lip. Wow, his head was pounding.

"You better answer me, you are fucking asshole. I hate you!" Deena stated regretfully. Her whole world was falling apart.

"The same time and day you go to see yours," Aiden stated as he began to laugh uncontrollably.

The entire room was in shock. Aiden and Deena were cheating on each other. Aiden knew about it? Deena looked at the confused faces. She smiled apologetically at her husband's bloody face. Deena broke free of the men and ran to his side.

"Oh, baby, I'm soooooo sorry," Deena stated as she began to nurse her husband.

Chase witnessed the interaction between the couple. Chase wondered how in the hell he was so calm. He had to know he was busted. Chase grabbed the arm of his chair tightly. It took everything in him to stay in his seat. He wanted to kill Aiden right now for being a manipulator, hypocrite, preaching God's word and loving his wife and all those other women.

"Dammit, Aiden, you almost had me. I was enjoying the newfound closeness with my wife. I was mending and cutting back on the adulterous affairs with the other women. But your muthafucking ass is out here fucking all those women and coming home to your wife and acting like you love her. It's preachers like you that keep men like me from the church. You ain't nothing but a man that uses your pulpit power to get you some ass!" Chase yelled as he stared Aiden in his eyes.

Deena watched Aiden as he laughed uncontrollably.

"Deena, have you gone mad? You are a psychologist, and you need your head examined. What's going on with your family that both of you are cheating?" Katherine Gregory had heard and seen enough of this.

"Picture's don't lie," Katherine spewed out.

"Babe, I think we better tell them," Deena stated, trying to clean up his face. Aiden agreed as he tried to get up.

"I have been having an affair. Yes, Constance, every Thursday at the hotel, before Marrytude - with my wife Deena. My baby is a lady in the sheets and..." Deena cut him off. Aiden winked at the other men.

"I confess. I have been, too! With my husband." Deena smiled as she continued to assist her husband remove the blood from his face
.

"But the pictures. And the other women?" Constance stated, still confused.

Deena smiled. "Constance, they are disguises, and its role play. Maybe you should try it. Chase won't ever stray again." Deena smiled. Constance hung her head down.

"I'm sorry. I almost destroyed a relationship because I thought it was a replica of mine. I wanted so much to rid myself of the gossiping. I allowed myself to get caught up in somebody else's business. I could have destroyed the church and marriages," Constance explained.

Aiden was helped off the floor by the two men. Pastor Gregory was relieved that Aiden was not a hypocrite. Chase had no idea that a man in the Word of God could have a sexy relationship like that, and with his wife. Chase thought he could learn some pointers from Aiden. Aiden had restored his faith in true men of God.

"Constance, it was not your fault. Whenever we have to deal with an issue where we have been fighting to keep our spirituality, there are often tests we have to pass. Did it look like I was cheating? Yes. It didn't help that my wife likes to yo yo diet and wear costumes. Even I as a pastor have to not show the appearance of evildoing. Maybe it was not wise to be down the street from the church, but it just added excitement to our role playing," Aiden reasoned.

"It takes time to get there. I'm proud of you, Constance. You sought out wise counsel, used wisdom, you will conquer gossiping. I love you in Christ," Aiden stated as he felt a deep pain in his side. Constance smiled.

"Deena, I think I have a cracked rib, take me to the hospital," Aiden stated, out of breath. Deena quickly retrieved their things.

"Deena, you're pretty quick. If ever I'm in an alley, I want you to be my bodyguard," joked Chase.

"Chase, I think you will be just fine. Your bodyguard, with a little more training, will be even better than me." Deena winked at Constance as she left the room with the only man who infused her with the energy to make it through the week, her lover for life, Pastor Aiden Michaels.

The best men are from the God of Abraham. A good man is hard to find, but one that believes and follows the word of God will forever cherish and honor his wife. A husband crafted and perfected by God, priceless.

EXCERPT FROM

3 SUM

COMING 2018

3 Sum

The Train

Andre stared at the barbells in the stand. He was angry. He could not believe that his wife of ten years had betrayed him. He continued to lift. He understood that a woman needed love. He spent his time showering his wife with gifts. He was sensitive to her needs, and she had an affair with a teenager in college. Damn, he thought. He should have listened to his mother when she had asked him if he was sure she was the one. During the course of the marriage, he thought about cheating. Hell, what man did not? But because he honored his vows and took marriage seriously, he had not.

Andre tried to spice up the marriage bed, but she refused. He understood now why she was a prude, she had a hot young male body while he slaved clocking over 60 hours a week working to give his wife the good life. As he finished and placed the barbell back into its base, he glanced at the television. Andre's one great love was on the entertainment show. She looked stunning. There was not an ounce of bitterness. He remembered the first time they had met. She took his breath away. She was dressed in white, and he was mesmerized by her presence. She had not changed. He wondered why she was interviewing on television.

"Excuse me, do you know why she is on television?" The lady looked at him strangely.

"You don't know? That's January Travis! She is the hottest sex therapist in the world. She just wrote her latest steamy novel for couples, called *Fun in the Bedroom*," she reported excitedly.

Andre smiled, his one great love had become successful. He thought she would never get over the pain of the abortion he made her have eighteen years earlier. He made it a point to be at her book signing tomorrow. He smiled as he got into his car. How fitting she would be a sex therapist. Sex was always great and experimental between them. He wondered if she ever thought about him the way he thought about her...he wondered if she still had feelings for him.

January was amazed at how many people loved sex. She was able to pick up the pieces of her life and create a nice empire. She went down the steps of the huge bookstore and began signing her book.

She smiled, and thanked the people for purchasing her literary work. January's hands were tired. Hopefully, she prayed this was the last one. She looked up, and Anthony winked at her. The wink was always their signal that this was the last group of people. It usually meant ten more to go. January glanced up to see her literary agent beaming. January assumed the book signing went well.

January took the book from the gentleman's hand without looking up.

"Good afternoon, sir, what would you like me to write?" January stated sweetly.

She still had that soft and sexy voice.

"Your name and phone number," he stated, hoping January would remember. She looked up and stared at Andre Garrison. For a brief moment, she allowed herself to remember the sweet lovemaking and kinky sex. She knew she turned him out. She stopped reminiscing because the next part was too hurtful to remember.

"Okay, if that is what you want," she stated as her eyes danced over his physique. "You have aged well." January smiled. "But I don't live there no more. Kind of have money now. I'm not living off no food. Remember you used to complain I never had food?" she stated jokingly. January realized she was talking too much. Damn, she thought. He always seemed to have that effect on her. Her hands started to shake. January took a deep breath and hoped he did not notice her nervousness. January thought, remain as cool as a cucumber.
Her eyes were kind, her composure was confident; if she still hated him, she did not show it.

Andre wanted to talk with her, tell her how he had made a mistake. It seemed like the rest of the crowd was getting restless, and a tall man from out of nowhere had nudged him to move on. After the book signing, Anthony stared at her.

"Are you okay? You have been quiet ever since you talked to that man who held up the line."

January smiled. "Of course I am. I'm just a little tired. I did not expect so many people. I mean, I'm happy, but just tired." She yawned as she pulled the covers around her and laid on Anthony's shoulder.

Anthony remembered the first time he saw January. She was buying a sandwich at the sandwich shop before she boarded the Amtrak train to California. Anthony teased January all the way to California. He used to work for the train company, and two years later this lady had changed his life. He was excited because she was going to help him direct a movie. She told him great things. January had not steered him wrong yet.

"Anthony, you ever had any thoughts about you and me?" January stated as she kissed his neck.

"Woman, don't you do that. I will attack you in this seat," Anthony stated.

"No, you won't. You are sweet and kind. You take good care of me." January yawned again and fell asleep. Anthony felt safe. If ever Anthony wanted to stop being the playboy, January would settle down with this nice looking young man. Anthony was going through a terrible break up, and January was finally ready for a real relationship. When she was not so tired, she would ask Anthony if they should hook up. The single lady life was playing out. January could not believe it: what, she wanted a relationship! January dreamed about Anthony. He was 30 years old, she was forty; it might be nice. She never had a young one before. He needed healing, and she was ready for a real relationship...maybe; stranger things have happened.

Anthony looked out the window as the train left New York City. January had been acting strange all day. Anthony thought about January's question. Any man in his right mind would love to make love to January. He was definitely included. January was a sex goddess. He could not tell her that, but he was a little shy around her. He watched her work her magic and leave men speechless at her assertive behavior.

"Hey, Anthony...I thought that was you. How's it going?" asked a car attendant named Lucas. Three years ago, they were co-workers on the same train.

"Going good, how's the family?" Anthony stated, thankful for the distraction.

"My wife saw you on the morning show, you looked like a movie star! I'm proud of you! And is that her?" He looked at the sexy female that was lying on Anthony's shoulder.

"She is so beautiful...wow, you are so lucky. So, are you and January together?"

"No, she's my boss. It's like I'm a little brother. She promised to teach me the business, and I'm learning a lot, she has not steered me wrong," Anthony stated as he and Lucas exchanged information.
"Maybe if we need some extras or something, I will call you. I remember Amanda had the acting bug."

January stirred as she heard the car attendant walk away. She reached over and put her hand on his lap. Anthony jumped.
"So, I treat you like a little brother? Why don't you want me?" January knew she had better stop. She saw the looks Anthony had given her over the years. For some reason, she had always known that Anthony was attracted to her, but he never played into her advances.
"Because, January, you don't want me, you still want Andre," Anthony stated as he got up and walked away.

The words stung as she heard the hurt in his voice. Was it that obvious? Did she really have a thing for Andre after all these years? When she saw him in New York City, her heart did skip a beat. But she had heard he had married some chemist or pharmacist. Ironic, she thought; she needed to follow her own advice and move on. Maybe January thought she owed Anthony an apology. That was something new; she did not know what to say.

They had 22 hours on this train. Maybe by noon, Anthony would return to his seat. She was not sure why Natalie did not give them the sleeping car. She began to fiddle with her laptop. Maybe if she wrote something steamy, she would figure out a way to tell Anthony she was sorry.

She looked at her phone. She had an unfamiliar text. She ignored it. Before she knew it, it was time for lunch. She wondered if Anthony would be eating lunch with her.

"How many, ma'am?" asked the lunch lady. January replied, "Just one." When they called her time for lunch, she saw Anthony laughing and joking with the staff. He ignored her. She sat down and began eating her meal. Midway between eating, another family joined January and they had a good lunch.

Anthony did not return to his seat until 3 pm. He did not know how to tell her he was sorry for his outburst. He hated seeing January in such turmoil. Hell, he hated seeing himself in turmoil. It had been six months, and he still thought about his ex-wife. He hoped he did not stay mad forever. He wanted January just as bad as she wanted him, but he had to be sure it was not just a rebound effect. He did not want to mess up the friendship they had developed by taking it to the next level. He had a work romance before. It did not work, and besides, he had seen how cold January can be when she was done with men after sex. January returned to her seat and smiled at Anthony.

"Look, I'm sorry; from now on, I will be good. I guess I just lost myself," January stated as humbly as she knew how.

Anthony looked at her with kind eyes. He nodded, and under his breath he said, "I'm sorry, too, but January, you are too sexy for words, you need to stop thinking about him, I know he hurt you. I see the tears every time you see a family, every time you see a mother and a father with kids, but he married someone else, he moved on, you need to also. Any woman would love to be in your shoes, you are making yourself sick, stop thinking about him," Anthony stated as he just let all his feelings out he had bottled up for two years.

January looked like she was going to cry. How could she tell this young man that it had become worse when she saw him at the book signing? Anthony looked at January. Oh damn, he had done it now. She was a basket case. The tears were welling in her eyes. She tried to fight back the tears. The conductor passed by. He was an old friend of Anthony.

"Man, what have you done? You got this beautiful lady crying. Ma'am, I can have him thrown off the train," he stated jokingly.

Wiping her tears, January playfully stated, "Yes, next stop." She was thankful for the staff that was very personable on this trip. They always seemed to make her journey complete. As a matter of fact, that was how she met Anthony. On the second trip, she flirted with him so bad, when she left and gave him her card, he thought it was just about sex. He called and was surprised that her business was legitimate

.

"January, that was the hardest thing in the world to do," Anthony replied as the conductor left.

"What was?" January asked innocently.

"Ignoring you and not talking to you. January, I love being in your presence," Anthony said as he searched her face. She was very beautiful. She had an oval face and almond-shaped eyes that were very inquisitive. When she looked at someone, she focused entirely on their face, body language, and all attention was on the person talking.

"I know; it did feel hard. It actually hurt. I'm sorry, even this old bag of bones can act like a brat sometimes, too." She smiled as she went back to pecking on her laptop.
Anthony thought by no means was she an old bag of bones. She could easily pass for a woman of twenty-five. She had no wrinkles, and she rode her bike religiously for exercise. She stopped typing. He thought she probably had writer's block. He took her hand in his and squeezed it tight. She looked up at him and stared into his blue eyes.

115

He wanted to tell her how he wanted her since the moment he laid eyes on her. He wanted her to know that he was attracted to her and would love to do some of the scenarios she described in her book.

January leaned over and whispered in his ear. "Anthony, stop looking at me like that. You're making me think wicked thoughts," she remarked as she let her tongue trace the outline of his ear. Anthony shivered as the sensation made his heart quicken. She continued ever so lightly and then kissed his neck. She went back to his ear and blew in it a little. "You taste sweet," she said as she smiled devilishly.

Anthony looked at her. Yes, he thought, everything in her book was correct, she knew exactly what she was doing. He would be in trouble. Anthony had awakened the animal in January. She stood up and retrieved the blanket from the overhead baggage area. She sat down and stared at Anthony with bedroom eyes.

"Why are you looking at me like that?" Anthony asked, trying to hide his manhood that was protruding through his pants. Damn, he should have stayed in the slacks. He had changed into his basketball shorts because they were more comfortable on the train.

"Because I've never been attracted to a younger man before, and I want you," she stated plainly.

She eyed him and looked at his crotch. "I'm sorry. I promised I would be good," she stated as she leaned over and whispered in his ear.

"Would you like me to take care of your situation?" she said as she kissed his cheek and nibbled on his earlobe. Anthony was excited! A woman his age would have been fearful. He wanted to say yes, but they were on a crowded train. But then again, he had to realize who he was with. He was in the presence of January Travis, sex therapist extraordinaire. Anthony shook his head yes.

"I'm glad you obliged," she remarked as she gave him some cover, and with her free hand she grabbed a lotion bottle out of the travel bag. She placed both hands under the cover and expertly unzipped his pants. Next, she rubbed the sex lotion on her hands, as if to warm them up so as not to give Anthony a chill. She then placed both hands on Anthony's penis and slowly massaged it. She slowly worked her hands up to the head, and then back down. Anthony felt like he was in pure heaven. He relaxed as her soft hands played a beautiful melody on him. He began breathing deeply as her hands massaged his inner thighs, his balls, and his penis. He began to place his hand under her breast and was trying to grab her breast and please her as much as she had pleased him in this moment. The lotion only added to his feelings of bliss. Damn, Anthony thought, if she was this good with rubbing him down, she was a femme fatale in the bedroom. Anthony tried to hold out as long as he could. In a minute, he exploded all over her hand. She simply pulled out a towel and wiped up the excess. She smiled, and Anthony sat there for about five minutes, trying to regain his composure. He finally excused himself to go to the bathroom. As he cleaned up in the bathroom, he felt good and happy. January was sexy. Now he had energy too last. It seemed like she had energized him.

January had returned back to her seat. She hoped Anthony was okay. She looked down at her cell phone and saw another strange text. Janie, baby, I never stopped loving you. I want you back. I'm sorry I hurt you.

January looked at the window. The tears began to well up in her eyes all over again. She had waited so long to hear those words; it could only be one person. It was the love of her life, Mr. Andre Garrison. She smiled half-heartedly. He always seemed to show up when things were going great or she was embarking on something new. She had to mask her feelings. She did not want to hurt Anthony. He was a great young man. She did not want to taint him. She was angry because she should have not given him a hand job. She smiled; he was very receptive, and his hand felt good on her boobs. January was sure Andre was lying again; that is what he always did best to her. This time, she was not falling for it. She texted him back. I'm sure you do baby...you say I'm the one, right? Or is that today?

"Hi," Anthony stated as he returned to his seat with a goofy look on his face.

January asked, "You okay?", hoping she didn't mess up their relationship.

"I'm great, thank you," he said and went to sleep. January was busy arranging her calendar when a young lady approached her.

"I'm sorry to bother you, but are you January Travis?" the excited young lady stated as she urged her to sign her book.

January smiled and graciously signed her book. The young woman talked on and on about how January had encouraged her to find her inner sexuality. Then the young woman said it was because of her she was able to get her wandering husband back, and she owed it to *Fun in the Bedroom*. January loved to hear stories like that. It made her work worthwhile. January exchanged information with her and asked if she could use her as a testimonial for future endeavors. The woman was excited.

Anthony whispered in her ear. "You think maybe one day that could be us?" he stated.

January winced. She hoped he did not get all lovey-dovey. "I don't know; we have to take it one day at a time." She had to figure out a way to see where Anthony's mind was. January wanted to be with someone, but he was much younger, her employee, and a great friend. Damn, she thought, once again she did not follow her own advice.

"OK, I won't push, but I would like to find out what life would be like with January Travis." There, he finally blurted it out.

"Well, aren't we a little bold? If all it takes is a hand job, imagine if we did all the tricks with bells and whistles…you would be mine for life," she playfully remarked.

"I think that can be arranged," Anthony stated, ready and willing to take a chance with January.

"Are you serious?" she inquired.
"Yes, I am. I figure we have both been hurt, we get along great, and we work together. We already do your lecture on the fact of the matter seminar. I think this could work," Anthony half-convinced himself.

"Okay, so what happens when I'm old and you still look young? Are you going to want to take care of me?" she asked.

Anthony looked at her crazily. "Why would I not? I do that now."

January had to agree. It made sense. She was not planning on marrying him, so this little arrangement might work out. "Okay, we have a two-day wait in New Orleans. You know what? I say if we are compatible in the bedroom, then it is on." She smiled as she went back to typing away on her laptop.

Anthony smiled. He was going to taste and please this exquisite woman. He did not care about her past; he was going to make her feel like a virgin in love all over again.

January watched Anthony as he squirmed in his chair. He began to fidget like an excited little boy. He excused himself and disappeared to the car lounge. January continued to work on her laptop, and her phone rang. "January Travis. Hi…it's been a long time," said a voice that brought back memories of old. She took a deep breath.

When she had no words, breathing always seemed to give her time to think before she responded.

"Hello," she stated quietly. Why was she so nervous? Anthony had left. She felt like a school girl with a secret crush no one knew about. There was a long pause on both ends. Andre did not know what to say. He hoped and prayed she did not hang up on him.

"You look good on television. You still look sexy, gorgeous, hot. I'm so proud of you," Andre stated, beaming.

"I was a little surprised you gave me your number. I thought your autograph would have cursed me out. I mean, I'm glad you gave me your number," he stammered as he searched for the words to talk with Jan. He wondered why she had not said a word. He could hear background noise. There was no real way to say that he had made a mistake. First, he thought, I will get to know her better. He did not know if she was attached, had children, or maybe she had many guys.

"So, are you still mad at me?" he asked.
"No Andre, I'm not. I never stopped loving you. It hurts though, you married someone else. I'm not bitter, though. I was for a long time," January stated as the tears began again.

"It really hurts when I tell you I'm pregnant, and you tell me you are marrying someone else. Then you say I'm trying to trap you, and now you tell me in a text the feelings are mutual," January quietly said. She had no animosity towards him. Maybe this was his way of letting go and releasing himself from the guilt.

"But Dre, I forgive you." This time, she felt released and free. She wiped her eyes on the tissue.

"So why did you call me?" she asked.

"Remembering how good it used to be between us. Hoping I could get the chance to share my world with you?" he shyly stated.

"My…aren't we bold in our old age?" January joked. He could tell she gave her funny smile.

"And you think I would say yes?" she asked.

"I'm praying you will. Are you still in the L.A. area?" he asked.

"Yes, I have a home on the beach."

"I will be in town next week. Can we meet for lunch or something?"
"All right, sounds like a plan, call me." And she hung up the phone.

She hung up just in time. Anthony came back with her hot tea and his M&Ms.

"So, was that Andre on the phone?" Anthony asked.

"So, does this mean our date in New Orleans is off?" he asked

"Oh no, it is definitely on, and we will be there tomorrow at 1:45." She smiled

Anthony breathed a sigh of relief. He knew he was skating on thin ice and he had a little bit of time to prove that he had what she needed. He wanted to know what Andre had said, but January would reveal it in time.

Finally, the train pulled into New Orleans. They retrieved their luggage and went to the hotel. Anthony tried not to seem so eager. January noticed his tenseness. She lightly touched his arm in the elevator. "Don't worry, I will be gentle, but first go get cleaned up, and we will meet in about an hour, OK? We will take in some sights," she said as she exited the elevator on her floor.

There was a knock at the door as she ran the water for her bath. January stared in disbelief. Andre Garrison stood there with her favorite powdered confection beignets from Café du Monde.
"How did you know I would be here? Even relaxed?" inquired January as she retrieved the bag from him.

"Baby, we are soul mates, I know when you are crying, happy, or sad," he stated as he embraced and kissed January. She melted in the arms that were once her security. She had to be strong. She prayed and asked the Lord to help her. It took her ten years to get over this man.

The phone rang; January unwrapped herself from his embrace and answered the phone.

"Hey, you!" was the bass voice on the phone. January smiled. God had a wonderful sense of humor! The pastor, Rev. Marcus Watson, was calling her.
"Hi," January stated breathlessly. He was a gorgeous, dark chocolate man. He was 6'2" and had a six-pack that was exquisitely beautiful! She was so busy dreaming about him that she did not hear his questions. January wanted him, but because he was a man of God, she would never, ever tempt him. God would punish her!!

"I'm sorry…what were you saying?" she stammered as Andre Garrison began to kiss the nape of her neck.
"January, we need to do a lunch. When are you coming to my church?" he asked.

"Now, you know I can't cross my sexual freedom lifestyle with the Word of God. Lightning will strike from heaven." January laughed.
On the other side of the phone, his laughter permeated through the phone.

"Seriously Jan, you think half the parishioners ain't having sex? They know who you are. You promised. Besides, I have this nasty young lady that sits in the front row with no panties on. I need you to come put her in her place," Marcus stated.

"Ah, darling, you can handle yourself. One of us has to stay holy." She smiled. He was the perfect Adonis of a male specimen. He, too, had been burned in a relationship. She had met Marcus at the beach when he was mourning the loss of his wife. He looked awesome. Their joke was, she was his cock blocker to all the females that were after him, and he would keep her holy.

"Jan, seriously, God told me to tell you He loves you. God has a man just for you. Stop the lifestyle you are living. You don't have to do what you're about to do," Marcus said as tears began to well in his eyes.
January's heart stopped. She hated when God would send messages through Marcus.

"He hurt you, and he steals your energy. He looks to you to give him the power to move on. Break him loose, Jan, it's time to stop going back to your past. It is all about your future, remember lot's wife."
January began to cry. Andre stopped kissing her neck as the door tapped insistently a third time. January tried to regain her composure as she swallowed her breath.
"Marcus, why are you calling me and telling me this right now?" she stated as she went to the door and Anthony was standing there with her beignets. Both men looked at each other as Marcus waited patiently on the phone.